UNTIL ONE OF US IS DEAD

ANDY RAUSCH

For Kristin with Love

ONE

Denny was only 51, but damn if he didn't feel twice that. The last few years had been hard, but somehow he'd survived. Or, more to the point, was surviving. And it was all because of Allie. It wasn't because he was tough, although he was, and it wasn't because of determination or some divine plan of a mystical, magical sky-daddy. No, it was her, plain and simple.

Sitting there in McDonalds, he watched her coloring on a print-out coloring page. It was a picture of a dog wearing a fireman's hat. Why would anyone want a dog to be a fireman? Denny had no idea. It seemed like dogs would be far more interested in lifting their legs to the hydrants than they would in putting out fires. He realized there were those Dalmations who were used by firemen – at least on TV – but he couldn't figure out what the dogs could possibly contribute to the proceedings. He watched the seven-year-old, leaning intently over her picture, coloring, careful to stay within the lines.

Seeing her coloring the dog's face brown, Denny said, "I think fire dogs are supposed to be white with black spots."

The little girl looked at him, scrunching up her face in

disapproval. "That's ugly. My dog is brown. His name is Charlie."

"He's got a name, huh?"

"He does," she said, looking down at the paper again.

There were many reasons Denny knew he was becoming an old man, ranging from his receding hairline, turning grayer by the minute, to his ever-increasing out-of-touch views on music and society. But chief among them was the way this little girl made him feel. He found that watching her color, as mundane as it was, was now equal to watching a movie or a Royals game. Even as a parent he'd never really felt this sort of enjoyment simply watching his kids do run-of-the-mill day-to-day kid stuff. It wasn't that Allie was different from how his kids had been; it was just that he'd become old enough – he preferred to think of it as *mature* enough – to relax and appreciate the little things.

Allie.

She was that little thing. Especially now that everyone else was gone.

Thinking of this, Denny turned away, staring absentmindedly out of the restaurant window. And it all came back to him. All the people he'd lost.

First there had been Timmy. Timmy was only 14 when he died. He was fatally injured in a high-school football game. Timmy's team, the Trojans, had been winning, largely because of Timmy's on-field heroics. He was having his best game ever. They were up 38 to seven in the fourth quarter. It was third down with just over four minutes to go. Timmy stepped back in the pocket, looking for someone to throw to, but no one was open. So he stood there a second too long and he took the hit. A hard bone-crunching hit. From the stands, his mother said it looked the same as any other hit. Denny couldn't say for sure because he hadn't been there. He'd been where he'd always been – in his cruiser, patrolling the city. But this hit had been different, and Timmy's neck was shattered. He crumpled to the ground like a discarded piece of paper and lay there, broken. Caroline said when the other players cleared the way for the coaches to examine Timmy, his body twitched violently, so much so that she could see it from where she was. And then he died, right there on the field.

Caroline was inconsolable. She'd witnessed something no parent should ever have to watch. After that, she was as broken as Timmy had been. She became something less; something of no use to anyone. She started to look at Denny differently, blaming him. He could see it on her face just as plainly as he could see the make-up she applied so liberally. When loved ones die, it's natural to search for someone to pin the blame on, and Caroline had found her patsy in Denny. Never mind that he was hurting, too. Never mind that he'd been absent only because he was out working to put food on the table. When Denny went to work the morning of the accident, he had no inkling he would never see his wife or son again. Timmy died. Caroline had lived, but not *really*. She had remained alive only in the most literal sense – she continued to breathe. But the truth was, she'd died that night, too. And Denny wasn't the only one who saw it. Their other child, Evelyn, saw it, too. And she felt it – felt *all* of it – the coldness, the disdain, the blame. Feeling her mother's undeserved hatred towards her, Evelyn turned it around and redirected it back towards her.

By the time Caroline died, both Denny and Evelyn hated her. There was no other way to put it. They both secretly wished she would die. Maybe not die, but at least go away for ever. And then she did die, which made things even more diffi-cult. Neither of them ever admitted their feelings about her to one another, but Denny knew they'd both felt it.

Evelyn was the one who found her. It had only been eight

months since Timmy's death. It was a warm June day. The sun was out, the birds were singing, and neighborhood kids were out riding bikes and playing catch. When Evelyn came home from her boyfriend's house to grab some things, she she found Caroline lying in a bathtub filled with red water, dead with both her wrists slit. After having just lost her little brother, finding her mother dead was an incredibly hard thing for a 16-year-old to endure.

Denny and Evelyn went to the funeral, the second they'd attended in less than a year, and they both sat there wondering what had happened to the life they had known previously. Both of them knew right then and there that it was gone. By this time, they were both tough enough – *broken* enough – that neither of them cried. Denny was aware that everyone's eyes were on him, watching to see him weep, but he didn't give them the satisfaction. Thinking about them judging him made him even angrier than he already was. But he didn't cry. It wasn't because he didn't love Caroline. No, never that. She had been his high-school sweetheart. The love of his life. He'd lost his virginity to her. She had been his everything. The fact was that Caroline – the only woman he'd ever loved – had already been dead for nearly a year. He didn't cry because he didn't have any tears left to shed; he'd already spent them.

He started drinking. Not one or two beers here and there, but a bottle of Jack every day, seven days a week. And Evelyn suffered even more as a result.

Denny should have taken time off work. Everyone told him to, but he didn't listen. He'd never listened. He'd been a hard-headed SOB all his life, and this was no different. Looking back on it, he now wished he'd taken the time off to care for his daughter. But he didn't. He was a fuck-up as a parent just as he'd been a fuck-up at everything else. Soon Evelyn was doing a smorgasbord of drugs and getting into trouble for things ranging from telling her principal to go fuck himself to vandalizing some random woman's car for reasons Denny never knew. None of it had made sense, and that fact now baffled him. How could he not have understood what she'd been enduring? Had he taken the time to consider her pain rather than dwelling on his own, he would have realized how damaged she was. But he didn't. He'd been a selfish prick.

This led to Evelyn moving out and staying with her aunt Patrice at 17. Within the year, she was pregnant. She'd still been doing drugs while pregnant – the doctors found heroin in her bloodstream – but somehow Baby Allie had come through it unscathed. But Evelyn didn't make it. In the end, it wasn't the drugs that got her. Evelyn, Denny's first child, forever his baby girl, died in childbirth.

Somehow her death caught him off guard, even after the other deaths. Somehow it was different. He'd been deeply sad when Timmy died. He'd certainly been affected. And when Caroline had died, well, that was what it was... She essentially died twice, the first one making it easier to cope with the second. And, truth be told, the alcohol had softened it some. But not with Evelyn. Not with his baby girl. Nothing could have prepared him for the immense pain and emptiness he felt. Even when they'd been fighting, he'd always believed things would be right again one day. There would be time. There was always tomorrow, right? Except there wasn't. They had run out of tomorrows.

Denny had always felt close to the kid. All of her life he'd spoken to her like an adult. He didn't know if that was good or bad, but it had always felt natural. And he'd never felt bad about it because she'd been more of an adult as a child than most of the adults he'd known. But none of that mattered now. Nothing mattered.

Or so he'd thought.

But then he realized there was one thing left that mattered. One person. There was that precious child. Baby Allie. Suddenly, with everything and everyone else in his life gone, Denny had managed, finally, to get his priorities straight. Unfortunately, Caroline, Timmy, and Evelyn weren't here see it. Denny stopped drinking. He stopped smoking. And he turned in his badge. He did it all for Baby Allie.

It hadn't been easy raising Allie by himself, but he'd managed. Denny had always believed himself good at things but when Allie came along, it became apparent pretty quickly that he was lacking in some areas. It also became obvious how much of the child-rearing had been done by his late wife. He'd always believed they'd been equal partners, but he saw now that was bullshit. Parenting was a tougher gig than he'd realized. But he kept working at it, trying to provide Allie with the best life he could. Somewhere along the way he learned how to parent, and he and Allie became a family. A small family, but a family nonetheless.

When she was two, Denny's mother had started babysitting for her. Allie always enjoyed going to grandma's because she said Grandma had the best toys. One day when Allie was there, his mother coined the name "Denny-Pa", which was a combination of his name and the word grandpa. At first Denny scoffed at the name, thinking it sounded ridiculous. But his mother kept using it, and eventually it stuck. Just like that, he became Denny-Pa. It was a goofy moniker, but it's who he was. He was Allie's Denny-Pa, and she was his Baby Allie.

TWO

Evelyn's death had been the hardest thing he'd ever dealt with. He was there in the waiting room when she died. It had been him and a couple of relatives, all on Caroline's side, and a few of Evelyn's druggie friends. No one knew who the baby's daddy was, so at least there hadn't been some young knuckle-head there to put up with. As he'd waited on news, Denny sat in silence, alternately leafing through women's magazines and watching *Judge Judy* with the volume down. There were many shows a person could watch on mute and still be entertained by, but *Judge Judy* wasn't one of them. So he waited, proud of himself for staying awake the entire seven hours. Then, finally, a doctor – a young middle-eastern woman named Khan (he remembered because the name made him think of the character from *Star Trek*) – came out.

Denny had always prided himself on being perceptive and being able to read people – an ability that served him well as a cop – but not now. This time, it was not an ability he enjoyed having. He knew something was wrong when he saw the doctor's face. She looked tired and she wasn't attempting to conceal the grimness. If she was, she was doing a piss-poor job. In addition, her blue scrubs were soaked with Evelyn's blood.

Denny's first thought was that the baby had died.

He rose to his feet. Seeing this, Khan came to him.

"Are you with Evelyn Davis?"

Denny said he was.

"Are you...?"

"Her father."

The doctor gave him a look of sadness that surprised him, even more so the thousand times he would later recall it. Generally doctors became steely after having delivered bad news hundreds of times, but not her.

"I'm sorry," she said, looking like she was on the verge of tears.

That told the story, didn't it?

"I tried everything I could, but Evelyn didn't make it."

Despite knowing it would be bad news, he still wasn't prepared, and it hit him like a brick to the head. Denny had always been a tough guy; the guy who never let anything get to him and, if he did, he didn't show it. But not then. No sooner had the words left the doctor's mouth than Denny was doubled over, crying uncontrollably.

As understandable as it was that he'd felt that way, Denny would always feel embarrassed by his showing vulnerability. He'd been so overcome with shock and grief that the doctor had actually put her hand on his back to console him. She just kept saying: "I'm sorry, Mr Davis, I really am." Over and over, different variations of "I'm sorry".

Denny was sorry, too. He was sorry for everything he'd ever done or said to Evelyn. But even more so, he was sorry for the things he hadn't. The countless school events he'd missed. The high-school plays he'd foregone in favor of work. Caroline had told him Evelyn was a good actress, but he'd never seen her perform. Thinking back, he would always remember how happy she'd been to inform him that she'd been cast as Stella in *A Streetcar Named Desire*. She'd been giddy, talking a hundred words a minute. Despite her pride and enthusiasm, Denny still hadn't attended the show. He'd always figured that she and Timmy would understand his missing these things because he was working. The concept of taking time off work for them had never even crossed his mind. Looking back, he still saw practicality in this, but he also saw how his children would have remembered him, had they lived. The empty seat at the most important events of their lives would be the thing they would have remembered.

But it didn't matter. None of it mattered. They didn't think that anymore. They didn't think anything. And if they were somehow in some heaven somewhere, he doubted he would be something that even crossed their minds. The truth was, they hadn't known him, and he hadn't known them. Not really. He'd always believed he'd known Evelyn, that they were close, but the reality was that they weren't. How could you be close to someone you never saw? This was why long-distance relationships rarely worked, and in those, the parties involved still spoke or corresponded more than Denny had conversed with his children.

So, when Evelyn died, Denny had set his sights on trying to correct these things. While he knew he could never truly fix any of it, he figured he could redirect his after-the-fact desire to be a good dad into taking care of Baby Allie. Caroline's sister, Kristine, had begged him to allow her and her husband Ray take the baby. "You can come see her whenever you want, Denny," she'd said. But Denny refused. He'd always been a mission-oriented guy, and he saw this baby as his latest mission. For a time, he'd worried that Kristine and Ray would try to take Baby Allie away, but they never did.

Denny and Allie became much closer than he'd ever been with his own kids. But Denny wasn't just closer to her than he'd been with them; he was closer with her than he'd ever been with *anyone*. He'd never had many friends, and that had been by design. He'd always been a loner. But not anymore. Now Allie was his everything. She was his best friend and his entire life.

He'd gotten by without working much. He worked part time as a short-order cook at Tommy's Diner in the mornings while Allie was at school, and they had managed to scrape by thanks to the respectable stock portfolio Caroline had accumulated before her death. The funny thing was, Denny had no idea how much money there was until after she was gone. He'd been pleasantly surprised, to say the least. He'd felt bad about using the money at first, but eventually came to accept that Caroline was gone and couldn't use it.

Denny and Allie went to the park and played games like Mr Dinosaur. Allie had invented this game, and it was her favorite. It was a game where she pretended Denny was a dinosaur. She was very exact about the type of dinosaur he was, too. She'd explained that he had to be a Velociraptor, as that was her favorite dinosaur. He would chase her around and she would scream. Sometimes she would battle Mr Dinosaur with a stick, wielding it like a sword. Other times, she would ride on his back and scream out: *"Go, Mr Dinosaur, Go!"*

She made him feel young again, although his body reminded him otherwise. Especially after the times she rode on his back.

He and Allie developed a few traditions along the way. One was the bedtime story. When he would tuck her in at night, she would demand a bedtime story. The two of them, over time, created a character who would inhabit most of these tales. This had started with Allie asking: "What if there was a man who had a gerbil head?" The thought of this had started her giggling uncontrollably. When she said that, Denny envisioned someone with a man's body, wearing clothes and shoes, but with a gerbil's head on top. He'd described this, and she'd agreed that it was perfect. "What should we name him?" he'd asked. Allie had dutifully considered this, and had then said, "Tom. His name should be Tom." Denny had asked her why, to which she simply replied: "Because it's a good name." Denny had said fair enough, and Gerbil Head Tom was born. Each night in the years since, Denny would make up tales of Gerbil Head Tom and his trusty sidekick Monty Mongoose. Sometimes Tom and Monty would just hang out and get into trouble at school, and then in other stories they would have exciting adventures like traveling through time, going into space in a rocket made of aluminum cans, and even meeting the president.

Another Allie and Denny-Pa tradition was the utterance of a line. It had started one day when they were in the car in the bank drive-thru. Allie had asked: "Denny-Pa, how long will we be together?" Denny thought about it for a moment. "Until one of us is dead," he'd replied. After that, it became their routine. They would ask one another, "How long will we be together?" To which the other would reply: "Until one of us is dead."

Life was good. This year they had started to travel, visiting places and things within driving distance. Last month, they drove to the Ozarks to see some caverns Denny had read about. They had both been bored to tears by the caverns but had then gone on to Branson to an amusement park called Silver Dollar City. They'd had such a good time on the trip that they had now returned to the area, this time to go camping. They both had a good time. They hadn't done anything too eventful, but they had rented a boat and had gone fishing. It was the first time Allie had ever gone fishing. Denny had never cared much for it, but had done it on occasion as a younger man, more or less just sitting on the dock with a fishing pole and drinking beer. But he had decided to do it with Allie because it would be something new for her to experience. As it turned out, Allie didn't like fishing either. She'd been particularly disgusted with the experience of hooking a worm. "That's mean, Denny-Pa," she'd said. "That worm probably has a mommy and daddy who will miss her."

The trip had also been memorable because it had been the first time Allie had ever been on a boat. She really enjoyed the boat and liked sitting in the front and feeling the wind against her face as they moved forward. The funniest part had been when she had to pee. That was when she had the experience of peeing in the lake for the first time. She hadn't wanted to, but eventually she did it.

The night before they left, sitting beside the campfire, Allie had looked at him with sweet, soft eyes. "Denny-Pa," she said. "I love you more than anything in the whole world." Denny had looked at her, feeling incredibly moved, and said: "I love you more than anything, too." Allie being Allie, she then asked exactly how much he loved her. To this he said, "I love you eight million." He thought this would please her, but instead she frowned. *"Only eight million?"* she asked. He grinned. "You didn't let me finish. I love you eight million trillion billion." Her face lit up. *"Really?"* "Absolutely, baby girl." They sat there for another few minutes, Denny basking in the moment. Then Allie broke the silence. "Denny-Pa?" she asked. "Will you promise you'll never ever leave me?" He smiled. "I promise, baby. You and me will always be together." She looked at him, smiling, a knowing look in her eyes. "How long?" He smiled back. "Until one of us is dead."

THREE

They sat there in McDonalds for a long time, Denny eating his cheeseburger and fries, Allie coloring her fire dog. Having already colored everything in the picture that could be colored, she was now going back over it a second time. Denny thought she was overdoing it, but said nothing as he saw no harm in it. As she colored and scribbled, he looked around, observing the other customers. A lot of them were rednecks, and for reasons Denny did not understand, rednecks fascinated him. He didn't like them. He hated them, their politics, and what he perceived to be their simple ways, but they still fascinated him in the way that people who hate snakes still stand and gawk at them.

They were in a fairly small town called Rolla, smack dab in the middle of nowhere. Denny and Allie were just passing through on their way home from their camping trip at Table Rock Lake. Denny had wanted to wait another hour or so to stop and eat, but Allie had insisted.

"I'm hungry," she'd whined from the backseat. Denny loved the kid, but he'd found himself feeling a little bit annoyed. Willie Nelson and Merle Haggard were on the radio singing about

Pancho and Lefty, and Denny wanted to listen to the song in peace. It was a good one, a song he'd always enjoyed, and it was an oldie he rarely heard on the radio. He'd ignored the statement – really more of a demand – the first time, but was forced to respond when she said it again 30 seconds later. He looked in the rearview mirror, seeing her desperate eyes looking back at him.

"We'll get something soon," he said.

He could only see her eyes and the bridge of her nose in the mirror, but could still read anguish on her face. She had expressive eyes. He heard her sigh.

"I'm hungry nooooow," she said, stretching it out.

They were between towns at the moment. "Look around, baby," he said. "There aren't any restaurants here. We have to wait until we get to the next town."

This didn't convince her. As any parent knows, seven-year-olds don't care about such trivialities as logic or facts. They only care about what they know to be immediately true, and at that moment her immediate truth was that she was hungry.

"Please, Denny-Pa," she said in a pained voice that melted his heart.

He tried to convey understanding with his eyes but wasn't sure he was accomplishing it. And even if he had, she was seven, so he doubted she would recognize it. "We're gonna be to the next town in about five minutes."

"How long is five minutes?"

Good question. He considered it for a moment, finally giving her the flippant answer that it was "a minute longer than four minutes and a minute less than six". He knew this wouldn't appease her, but he'd said it only for his own amusement.

"What are we gonna eat?" she asked.

"I dunno, Allie. It depends on what they have."

"What *do* they have?"

He looked at her, seeing her staring back with a look that was somehow both angry and doe-eyed innocent.

"I don't know, baby. I don't know what they have."

"*Why?*"

He sighed, turning his attention back to the radio. He managed to listen to about 20 seconds of it before she interrupted. "When are we gonna eat, Denny-Pa? I'm hungry..."

"You're hungry, huh?" he asked, again for his own amusement. But she didn't know he was joking. Nuances were lost on seven-year-olds. Just after he'd said it, he saw a sign advertising a McDonalds four miles away.

WHEN THEY GOT TO McDONALDS, Allie was acting as if she might die of starvation at any moment. Had he not known better and could only hear her whine about her hunger, Denny would have believed he was listening to one of the bony malnourished African kids from that old Sally Struthers commercial.

"What do you wanna eat?" Denny had asked, knowing full well what the answer would be.

"Chicken nuggets," she said. It was always chicken nuggets. Every single time. And yet he continued to ask for reasons he didn't understand.

That had been 40-some minutes ago, and the two of them were just sitting there in the booth.

Allie looked up. "I need a new coloring paper."

"Why?"

"Cause this one's all colored up."

She raised it to show him. He looked at it, seeing that it was indeed "all colored up".

"Tell you what, kiddo. How about I go to the restroom real quick, and then we go."

"Back on the road?"

"Back on the road."

"I don't wanna get back in the car."

"We can't stay here."

"Why?"

"It's McDonalds. People don't live in McDonalds."

"I mean the town. We could stay in a motel."

"Motels cost money."

The little girl thought about it and then said, "We have our tent in the car. We could sleep in that."

"We don't know anyone here," he said. "And in a few hours we'll be back home and you'll be able to sleep in your own bed. You can sleep under your My Little Pony blanket and snuggle with your teddy bear. Won't that be nice?"

Allie sat there for a moment, considering it. Finally she did a half-shrug and said, "Okay, but..."

He looked at her.

She asked, "Number one or number two?"

"What do you mean?"

"Do you need to go pee or do you need to go poop?"

Denny grinned. "Why do you need to know?"

"I just do."

"Number two, OK? You happy now?"

She nodded. "Sure. But one thing."

"What?"

"What am I gonna do while you're gone? I'll be bored."

He smiled, trying not to appear condescending. "Color some more. There's a little space there on the edges of the page where you can still color."

She frowned.

"And if you sit here and be a good girl for the next three minutes, I'll buy you a shake before we go."

Suddenly, Allie brightened, sitting upright. "Chocolate?"

Getting to his feet now, Denny said, "Sure thing. Anything for my baby."

As he turned to go to the restroom, Allie frowned. "I'm not a baby! I'm seven!"

"Sorry," he said. "I'll be right back."

"Okay, Denny-Pa."

Denny walked over to a young pimply-faced McDonalds employee sitting in the lobby, obviously on his break. "Hey kid," he said.

The kid looked at him with a "what the hell?" look.

"Tell you what," said Denny. "I gotta go to the restroom. It's just me and my kid there, and I don't wanna leave her out here alone." Denny motioned toward Allie, still looking down at the coloring sheet. "I'll only be a couple minutes. If you watch her while I'm in there, I'll give you five bucks. Whaddaya say?"

The kid looked over at Allie and then back at Denny. "I'll do it for 10."

Goddamn kids, Denny thought. "OK, 10 it is."

The kid nodded and Denny went to the restroom.

DENNY MOVED AS QUICKLY as possible, finishing the entire process in less than five minutes. He went to wash his hands but found the soap dispenser empty. "Shit," he muttered, rubbing his hands together beneath the running water, sans soap. When he finished, he turned to the paper towel dispenser, finding it empty as well. "Great," he said to himself as he pulled the door open.

As he walked down the short hallway towards the foyer, he

remembered that Allie wanted a shake. Maybe he would get one, too, he thought. When he walked into the foyer, he looked across the room to where Allie had been, but didn't see her. He looked where the kid who said he'd watch her had been, but he was gone, too. *Christ*, he thought. He scanned the room, searching for Allie. At first he thought maybe she was beneath the table, playing. But she wasn't. His heart started to beat harder and his throat tightened. He moved towards the counter, seeing the kid behind it, milling around with a heavyset female employee.

The kid looked up at him.

"Where's Allie?" asked Denny.

"Who's Allie?" the kid asked.

"My little girl. The one you're supposed to be watching."

"Oh, yeah. Sorry, man. I had to go back to work. Steve, my manager, came out and told me to get back here so he could take his break."

"OK, so where's Allie now?"

The kid showed his stupidest face and shrugged. "I don't know." As he said it, Denny could see his eyes scanning the room.

Denny was angry now. He pointed at the kid. "*She better not be lost,*" he growled.

The kid jumped a little, looking frightened. "Hey, you don't have to worry about paying me," he said.

Denny glared at him. The kid cowered a little, and Denny turned back towards the lobby. As he did, he heard the female employee say, "What's his deal?"

Maybe Allie had gone to the restroom. Yes, that had to be it, he thought. So he went to the women's restroom. When he got there, he stood there for a moment, trying to figure out what to do next. He reached for the handle, but the door opened before he touched it. A middle-aged woman who smelled like she'd spilled perfume on herself stepped out, looking at him, wondering why he was in her face.

"Did you see a little girl in there?"

She looked confused. "A little girl?"

"In there," he said, pointing.

She was still confused.

"Jesus Christ, lady. It ain't that hard."

"No," she managed. "No little girl."

Shit. He turned back towards the foyer, his heart racing. His feet were moving, but he didn't know where to go or what to do. He looked around the room, now seeing a large woman sitting with her family staring at him. He approached her. "Did you see my little girl?"

"The one who was sitting with you?"

"Yeah. Did you see her?"

"Yeah, I saw her."

He was growing impatient. "Did you see where she went?"

"The little redhead girl?"

Denny lost it. *"Yes, goddammit, the little redhead girl! The one sitting at my table! Did you see where she went?"*

The woman looked offended. She paused for a moment before pointing at the exit. "She went out there."

His heart was in his throat. "Was she alone?"

"No, she went with the man."

Denny was pissed. Pissed at the world, not this woman, but he took it out on her anyway. *"What fucking man?"*

The woman sat there, looking around, first at him and then at the door, her mouth agape.

He stepped towards her, growling, *"Tell me!"*

"The fat man," she said.

Denny turned, moving now, quickly, towards the door. Before he reached it, his eyes were already scanning the little bit of parking lot he could see. He burst through the doors –

there were two of them – stepping out into the fading sunlight, looking both ways. There was no one there except a young female employee with blue hair who looked like a drug addict, sitting on the ground with her back against the building. She was smoking a cigarette, paying him no mind.

He was about 10 yards away from her. *"Hey, you!"*

She looked at him.

"Did you see a fat guy come out here with a little girl?"

The girl nodded. "Yeah, I saw 'em."

"Where'd they go?"

"They left."

Denny was terrified. He looked around as he asked, *"Where? Where did they go?"*

"Hell if I know."

"How long ago?" It was a stupid question and he knew it. The whole thing had occurred in less than 10 minutes.

"I don't know," she said. "Couple minutes, I guess. I wasn't really paying attention."

Fuck. What was he gonna do now?

"Are you sure a fat man and a little girl just left together?"

"Yes," she said, sounding annoyed.

Denny lost it again. He looked to the sky and stamped his feet, screaming out: *"Fuuuckkk!"*

The girl just stared at him. He looked at her again. "OK, did you see what the man was driving?"

"Yeah," she said. "Normally I wouldn't have paid any attention, but he had a dumb bumper sticker. It said JESUS IS MY BEST FRIEND. I just thought it was really moronic, so I noticed it when I came out here. I thought, who the hell would put that shit on their vehicle, you know? Then they came out and I knew."

"Knew what?"

"Whose bumper sticker it was."

Denny stood there a moment, lost and confused, his mind racing. He looked at her. "Did you see what kinda car he had?"

"It was a van. A really ugly little van. It looked... *old*. Really old."

"What color was it?"

"Blue."

"What shade of blue?"

"Shit, man," she said, sounding irritated again. "I don't get paid enough to answer all this. Besides, I gotta get back to work."

"It's the last question, I promise. What color was it?"

She shook her head. "I dunno. Blue. Just blue."

"Light blue or dark blue?"

"Light blue, I guess."

Denny stood in the parking lot, getting angrier and angrier, his world spinning. He watched the girl flick her cigarette butt on the ground and go back inside. As he stood there, his fists clenched by his side, he thought of the asshole kid who was supposed to watch Allie. His blood pressure was surging, his temples throbbing, and he suddenly saw red. *Goddamn him*, he thought, losing it. He turned and bolted towards the restaurant, going for the kid.

FOUR

Denny's head was spinning. Having been a cop for two decades, he knew there was nothing he could do. He was sitting there, alone in the police station, waiting in the detective's office. The guy's name was Jennings. He was nice enough, but he'd lectured him about attacking the kid. Thankfully Denny had only grabbed the kid, slamming him against the wall and screaming at him. "You're damn lucky they didn't press charges," Jennings had said.

"That kid was scared to death," Denny said. "He wasn't gonna press charges. You shoulda seen the look on his face. He looked like he was gonna shit himself."

"You sound proud of yourself."

"No, I'm not proud of myself. But I'm also not feeling bad about myself like I would have if I hadn't grabbed the little fucker."

"I'll bet you were a great cop," Jennings said dryly. Denny looked at him, now beyond giving a fuck. "I *was* a good cop. But I also did what had to be done."

Jennings then chose to change the subject, which Denny

believed to be a good thing for both of them. Instead, he'd left the room to get an update on what was happening. As Denny sat waiting, he felt himself starting to hyperventilate. He'd never been prone to panic attacks, but he felt like he was on the cusp now.

Jesus H Christ.

He stood, turning towards the door. He walked out, into a larger office that contained several desks. There was a female officer standing to his right, looking over some papers. She looked at him. "Jennings'll be right back."

"It's OK," he said, trying to remain calm, wanting to conceal how much he was freaking out. "I just need to get some fresh air."

She made a concerned face, conveying empathy. "You OK?"

"I'm..." What was the word? He didn't know. Finally he said, "Alive." He knew the word choice was weird in terms of conversation, but it was also the only one that seemed adequate.

"You'll be back?" she asked.

"I'll be right back."

She nodded, saying nothing else, and he moved past her.

When he stepped out onto the sidewalk, he looked around. He took a deep breath, the influx of oxygen making him feel tired. It didn't change anything else. His heart was still racing. He went to his car, parked there on the street. He got in, started it up, and drove to a convenience store, where he bought a pack of smokes – his first in years.

After he'd returned and smoked two cigarettes remarkably fast, he went back inside. He made his way to Jennings's office. When he walked in, Jennings was standing behind the desk, his back turned.

When Denny asked if there was any news, Jennings

jumped a little, startled, clearly unaware he was behind him. He turned around, holding some papers. Denny had no idea if the papers had anything to do with Allie, but figured they didn't.

"Not really," Jennings said grimly. "The McDonald's had surveillance cameras, but they weren't on."

This was not the news Denny wanted to hear.

"Why not?" he asked.

"Apparently they've been broken for a while."

"You're kidding."

Jennings slouched a bit, looking tired. "I wish I was."

"OK, so there had to be other cameras in the area. Businesses. Maybe a bank. I think there was a bank down the street."

"First Federal."

"Someone must have caught this bastard on film, right?"

"We're looking into it, but I'm not holding my breath."

Denny didn't understand. "What do you mean?"

"This isn't Kansas City. We're a small town. We don't have the resources you're used to. The truth is, a lot of the businesses here don't have cameras."

Denny shook his head. "I figured there were surveillance cameras everywhere."

"Not here," said Jennings. "We don't even have traffic cameras."

"*None?*"

"Not a one."

"OK, so what else?"

"We've got police all over the state looking for this guy, but you know the deal."

"What do you mean?"

"We don't have much to go on."

"We know what he looks like and what he drives. That should be enough."

Jennings gave him a look of pity. He sighed. "Think about what we have. It's very vague. We know he's a fat man and he drives a van. That doesn't tell us much. We don't even know exactly what 'fat man' means here."

"I don't follow."

"The girl who worked there and the two customers inside gave completely different descriptions. Somehow no one could remember what the guy looked like or exactly how big he was. One guy just said, 'pretty fat'. That doesn't help much."

"No one remembers what he looked like?"

Jennings shook his head. "I'm afraid not. Out of the two customers who even remembered seeing him, one thought he might have been wearing a hat and the other didn't think he was. Apparently, he was a very plain, nondescript guy. The fella I talked to described him as looking like a generic white guy. Those were his words, 'generic white guy'."

"OK, then. The van – what about that?"

"That's not real helpful either. All we know is that it was a van and that it was some shade of blue. The girl who gave us the description kept changing her mind about what shade it was."

"She wasn't real bright."

"No, she wasn't."

"I'm pretty sure she was on drugs."

"Oh, I guarantee it," said Jennings. "Meth. It's everywhere here. You can't throw a rock without hitting 10 meth-heads. But meth-head or no, she was the only one who saw the van. And given what we know about her, the way she looks and the way she acts... I wouldn't say her description is the most reliable. But then, even if she was right, we have no idea what make or model it was. That just leaves us with the description 'blue van'.

Do you have any idea how many blue vans there are in Missouri?"

"OK, but the bumper sticker."

Jennings nodded. "That narrows it down some. It's still gonna be tough to find. But we're hopeful."

Denny just sat there, trying to think of something new to say, trying to find some clue or solution that would crack the case.

"Look Mr Davis, the best thing you can do right now is go get some rest," Jennings said. "We've got your number. We'll call you when we've got news."

"You know I can't do that. I can't leave my baby... I... I can't leave her out there with that man... God only knows what he's doing..." Denny shuddered at the thought. He stood there in silence, thinking for a moment, and then looked up. "I'm staying here. In Rolla. I'll be here until we find her. I'm not giving up."

"I'm not asking you to give up. No one is giving up. It's only been a few hours. I'm sure we'll find them, but for now you should try and get some rest. You'll end up with an ulcer, and that won't do anybody any good."

"I've already got ulcers. You forget, I was a cop."

Jennings smiled an awkward, knowing smile.

DENNY STAYED in Rolla for the better part of a month, waiting for the fat man and Baby Allie to turn up. As he waited, he cruised the city, looking up and down each street for blue vans with bumper stickers. He occasionally found blue vans – he found a handful – but none of them had the bumper sticker. The thought occurred to him that the man could have removed the sticker, but he didn't know what else to do. He had also considered investigating each person who had a blue van on the off chance it was them, but in his heart he believed the fat man and Baby Allie were somewhere far away now.

The police didn't find either of them and, when Denny ran low on money, he was forced to return home. Detective Jennings assured him the police would continue their search, but both men knew the truth. As they spoke, Denny could think of little beyond the reality that the search was over. Denny believed Jennings was genuinely affected by Allie's kidnapping, but he also knew that police had too much work and far too little funding and manpower to search for ever. When the conversation concluded, Jennings closed by saying, "I'll keep looking, Mr Davis. I promise." Denny knew the detective wanted the statement to be true, but he also knew it wasn't. Maybe there would be fliers out there, and maybe Allie's picture would appear on a few missing-kid websites, but she had already become yesterday's news.

As the days and months passed, it became ever more apparent that she wasn't coming home. And Denny couldn't keep himself from considering the reality that his Baby Allie might be dead somewhere. He tried to push it from his mind, but the thought refused to leave.

Sometimes when Denny saw overweight men in public, he irrationally wondered if they were the guy. Once, in Costco, he became convinced, for no good reason, that a fat man wearing a baseball cap was Allie's kidnapper. He'd followed the man around the store, careful to keep his distance, and then out to the parking lot, where he found that the man was driving a Toyota. Seeing this, Denny just stood there, his heart heavy, watching the man drive away.

Allie had been gone for four months when her eighth birthday arrived. It was a sad day for Denny, the saddest he'd ever known. It was sadder than the deaths of his family because he now felt the pain of all their deaths combined, as well as the loss of the little girl who had been his last chance for redemption. In mourning Allie's loss, he was mourning all their losses.

He gave serious consideration to suicide. He sat in his recliner, holding his pistol for more than an hour, staring at it through blurry, tear-filled eyes. The truth was that he wanted very badly to end it all. But he couldn't. Despite the incredible, overwhelming emptiness he felt, he found himself too afraid to do it. This realization made him even more sad and he somehow felt like he was letting Allie down all over again. He knew it didn't make sense, that none of it was true, but it didn't change him from feeling that way.

Denny hadn't touched a drop of alcohol in eight years, but he started drinking again. That was the night he replaced Allie's presence in his life with that of his old friend Jack Daniels. And they became closer than they had ever been before.

FIVE
THIRTEEN YEARS LATER

THE YEARS since Allie's disappearance had not been kind to Denny. Mainly because he had not been kind to himself. After it had become clear she was really, truly gone, he had attempted to drink himself into oblivion. And it mostly worked. His body and his mindset had deteriorated significantly as a result, but he remained technically alive, much to his chagrin.

He'd spent those first few years – he no longer knew how many – searching high and low for her. These searches had yielded no results.

Once, when he was at a gas station somewhere near St Louis, Denny had spotted a "JESUS IS MY BEST FRIEND" bumper sticker on a yellow Honda Civic. Obviously he knew the owner wouldn't be the guy who kidnapped his granddaughter, but he'd approached the vehicle anyway. It turned out the driver was an elderly woman with a puppy in the passenger side. When he'd asked her where she'd gotten the sticker, she'd told him she'd ordered it from a Christian magazine. "You should get one," she'd advised, then adding, "I've seen quite a few of them. They're really neat, you know? They tell it like it is. People think Jesus is just some mysterious figure they never see, but really, he's with us all the time. He really is our best friend." To this, Denny had just muttered about it being bullshit and returned to his vehicle. Denny wasn't an atheist or an agnostic, but he didn't give a damn about a deity who could allow a seven-year-old child to be taken without consequence. The deaths of his wife and children hadn't left him feeling particularly close to God, but Allie's disappearance had sealed the deal. God was not Denny's best friend.

This was typical of his post-Allie mindset. He'd become bitter and hard; harder than before. If Caroline had thought he was a bastard when she was alive, she would have hated him now. Everyone in their right mind would have. A couple years back a woman named Dawn who lived down the street invited him over for dinner. He'd gone and they'd seen each other a few times after, but Denny never allowed himself to think of her as anything remotely meaningful. Not even a friend. He wasn't sure why he'd seen her in the first place, but believed it was likely some inner longing for normalcy. But Denny wasn't normal. He would never be normal again. So, he'd said or done something to hurt her feelings and she had disappeared as quickly as Allie and the others had. He no longer remembered what he'd said or done, but it had done the job.

Marshall Hansen, a guy he'd known since high school and had been on the force with, had come by a couple times to see him. He acted warmly as though they'd always been friends, but that wasn't the truth. They'd never been friends. Denny had always felt disdain towards Marshall, and he'd always believed Marshall felt the same way. True or not, Denny couldn't know. But he'd been suspicious of Marshall's motives. Did he really care about Denny, or was he just looking for dirt to share with the other cops? It didn't matter, but Denny was curious. Either way, Denny had been less than friendly, probably saying something unpleasant – again, he no longer remembered – and Marshall stopped coming by.

Most days Denny sat alone in his dark house, curtains shut, staring at the television and drinking himself unconscious. Then he would sleep, wake up, and start the whole process again.

Denny hated his life, and most of all he hated himself. The thought of his letting Allie down haunted him. It was like a shadow, always there, always with him. He would stare at himself in the mirror – the fat, unhealthy, unshaven loser he'd become – and wish death upon himself. Oh, how he longed to die. Yet he didn't have the balls to do it. Why was that? In the moments when he was lucid enough to consider such things, Denny would ask himself that question. The answer he arrived at most frequently was that he was inflicting pain upon himself. Living, he felt, was a more torturous punishment than a bullet. He didn't deserve the bullet. He didn't deserve an easy escape. He deserved the pain. All of it. Every last bit.

Today was like every other day had been for many years now. He was sitting in the darkness, in his dust-covered living room, drinking Jack with the TV on. He was absent-mindedly watching men's curling on ESPN. He didn't give a shit about what he was watching, but then he didn't really care about anything these days. Just Baby Allie, and she was long gone and most likely dead.

Denny hated that realization, and he fought with it, pushing it away when he could. Some years ago, Caroline's sister Kris had called to suggest that a funeral should be held for Allie. "It'll be cathartic," she said. "It'll give you closure."

"I don't want closure."

She'd paused, then saying, "Well, the rest of us do."

And he'd replied: "It's not about you. None of this is about you."

"Then who's it about, Denny?"

"It's about Allie."

"Allie's dead. You have to face that. It's been a long time."

"She's not dead." He'd paused before adding, "Not to me."

Around this point in the conversation Denny had become aware that Kris was crying.

"She's not coming back," she'd said.

"You don't know that!" he'd screamed.

"Denny."

"There's not even a body. How do you have a funeral without a fucking body?"

"Please. Think about Caroline, Denny."

"You think I don't? I think about her every day. I think about all of them. They were *my* family, Kris. You know what? Those memories are all I have left. I hate them because they hurt like hell, but they're all I've got."

"Denny, listen, I need you to..." Denny had no idea what she'd said next because he'd interrupted, saying, "Never call here again," and hung up. Denny had no time or patience for niceties. Not any more. The whole world could go to hell for all he cared. His world already had.

So here he was, watching a bunch of Italians moving around a stone on ice, when the phone rang. He sighed, staring at the phone, feeling too tired to answer. Despite this, he did it anyway, out of some ingrained sense of responsibility.

"Hello?"

"Denny?"

"Yeah."

"This is Beverly."

Beverly was his sister. He said nothing.

"Are you there?" she asked.

"What do you need?"

"It's Daddy."

Denny hadn't thought about his father in years. He was frankly surprised the cocksucker was still around. "What is it?" he asked.

"He's dead. He had a heart attack."

Denny felt something deep down, but couldn't identify what it was. It wasn't pain in the way that he'd ever known it, and by this time he was well aware of what grief and pain felt like. He would later identify it as a different kind of hurt altogether. It was heavily numbed by alcohol, but it was pain nonetheless, his sorrow over his guilt for not caring. Some long-dormant conscience deep down inside him felt guilty for not caring that the man who'd brought him into the world was now dead. But really, Denny had never liked the sonofabitch.

As shocked as he was by these feelings, Denny found himself even more stunned by the sense of responsibility that led to his then traveling to attend the funeral. Denny didn't want to go. Not only would they be celebrating a man he'd passionately hated – a man who'd beaten both his mother and him, once even breaking his mother's collarbone – but he also didn't want to leave home. His life was terrible, but it was what he was comfortable with.

His father had been living in Stillwater, Oklahoma for the past decade, ever since his mother's death. Denny had seen his father crying at the funeral, and the sight of it had angered him. That was it. Afterwards, Denny told the old bastard how he felt, and the two of them never spoke again. Now they never would, and Denny was fine with that.

Denny was driving to Stillwater for the service, drinking from his flask as he did. The drinking didn't affect his driving. Now he was a functioning alcoholic, meaning he not only functioned well on alcohol, but absolutely needed it to function properly. The radio was on a classic rock station, and Denny was singing along absent-mindedly – not even realizing he was doing it – when he saw the gas station up ahead. He took a glance at his gas gauge, already knowing the tank was near empty.

He pulled into the lot, idling up beside the pump. He got out, fumbling for his wallet and then his card. As he did, he looked up and saw the light blue van sitting near the exit across the lot. It was an older model, probably 40 years old. He squinted, trying to see it better. At the angle it was, slightly off-kilter, he could see that it had a bumper sticker.

His breath stopped.

No. There was no way that was the van.

It wouldn't be it, he knew. It never was. Nevertheless, he had to know for sure. He climbed back into the car, moving it forward, edging out where he could get a better look. His eyes focused on the bumper sticker. As he edged closer, he could see the words.

JESUS IS MY BEST FRIEND.

Good Christ, was he really seeing this? Just as he realized he was indeed seeing what he was seeing, the van drove out on to the highway, going in the same direction Denny had been going. Shit. Denny had no choice but to follow. What should he do? Denny didn't know. He didn't have a gun. Was there anything he could use as a weapon inside the vehicle? Maybe there was a crow bar. He considered the possibility of just ramming into the van, forcing the guy off the road, and then beating the shit out of him. No, that wouldn't work. The main reason for this was because Denny knew he wouldn't stop at beating him. If he did what he needed to do in a place that was public, he would end up behind bars for the rest of his life. No, he thought. He would take his time and be patient. He would follow the bastard until he stopped somewhere.

Then he would play it by ear, figuring out his next move in the moment.

Fuck, he thought. He couldn't believe it. After all these years. This was the bastard who'd taken Allie. And then it occurred to him for the first time. It should have been his first thought, but it hadn't been: what if Allie was still alive? Denny had lived with the idea that she was dead for so long that his first thoughts had been vengeance rather than a reunion. This made him feel guilty, but it also gave him hope. It was the first time he'd felt hope in 13 years, and it frightened him.

DENNY FOLLOWED the van for another 10 miles, frightened he would run out of gas. Finally, when they reached a little town, the van pulled off on to a side street. It then went a few blocks, turning on to a back street. Denny followed at a distance. He saw the van draw up to the curb and park. In an effort to keep his presence a secret, Denny drove down the street a bit, parking against the curb. After shutting off the engine, he turned in his seat and looked out the back window.

He saw a heavyset man with a beard climb out of the van, going around the vehicle and up into the yard in front of a very rundown old house. The man went up on to the porch. He stood beside the door for a moment, removing mail from his mailbox. He looked at it for a moment, and then looked up. Denny was afraid he would look in his direction, but he didn't. The man then turned, unlocked the door, and went inside, closing it behind him.

This, Denny thought, was the moment of truth. This was when he would come face to face with the sonofabitch who had taken Allie and ruined and possibly ended both of their lives. He would have words with him first and then he would kill him. If things went right, he would find Allie and they would be reunited. He tried not to get his hopes up, fully aware this was a dangerous thing to do, but he couldn't help it. Denny got out of the car and went around it, unlocking the trunk. He rooted around inside it, searching for something to use as a weapon. He'd believed he might have a crow bar, but he didn't. There wasn't even a jack. Aside from an umbrella, there really was nothing that could be used as a weapon. And the umbrella would be a terrible one. He stood there for a moment, looking around, sort of lost, trying to decide what to do. As he did, his eyes fell to the brick sidewalk, overgrown and with most of its bricks cracked and broken.

Denny closed the trunk. He then walked towards the sidewalk, looking to make sure the man hadn't come back outside. He hadn't. Denny squatted down, searching for a loose brick. He didn't see any, so he plunged his fingers into the dirt along the side of one, working them into the ground. It took him a couple minutes to get the brick loose and then up from the ground, but finally he accomplished it. It was half a brick, which he could hold securely in his hand. A brick wasn't the ideal weapon, but it would do.

He walked towards the side of the house, thinking he would duck around back. That way he would be out of sight and could look for a way to gain entrance. He looked around, making sure there was no one to see him. There wasn't. He approached the side of the house. As he did, he saw a shovel leaning against its side. This immediately sent his thoughts into horrible places and he wondered if the man had used the shovel to bury Allie. This sent a chill running down his spine.

He shook it off, continuing to move towards the backyard. He came to the back corner of the house. He crept towards it, then carefully peering around. When he did, he saw there was no one in the backyard. The ground was muddy, and for some reason it occurred to Denny that his sneakers would be covered in mud.

He looked in the direction of the back porch. Maybe he could break into the back door, he thought. Creeping slowly, he heard a sound behind, startling him. He turned to see what it was, just in time to see the shovel for the split second before it struck him in the face.

SIX

The white light hanging overhead was the first thing Denny saw when he opened his eyes. It was blinding and bright, making him squeeze them shut again, then blink and squint. He heard music playing softly. It was *Alone Again (Naturally)*. His forehead was pounding. Where was he? He turned his head, looking around, now realizing something was askew. When he looked over, he found himself face to face with a gray brick wall. He heard the chains rattle. He looked at his hands, finding his wrists were shackled by thick black metal cuffs. He was taking all this in simultaneously, trying to understand. It all overwhelmed him, but the thing that stunned him most was the realization that he was completely naked, lying on a cold cement floor. He sat up, his tailbone hurting, pressed against the floor. He raised his hands, confused and frightened. The chains were heavy and thick, weighing him down. His heart raced, and he started to panic.

All this happened in a few seconds, and in that time Denny struggled to comprehend his surroundings. And then, suddenly, he remembered why he'd come. He remembered Baby Allie.

His heart was pounding and it felt as if it might leap out his chest. His eyes scanned the room, darting left then right, searching for answers. He was in was a basement. A rancid basement that smelled foul. What was the smell? Shit. And piss. And other foul, revolting odors he could not instantly identify. In that moment, he saw the blood stains on the walls and floor. The sight frightened him, and his breath caught. He forced himself to breathe, to focus but, before he could, he heard the man's voice behind him. "Good. You're awake."

Denny jerked, twisting his torso, his chains rattling, and he saw the man sitting on the floor with his legs crossed. He had a fat, round face, outlined with a beard that was blonde like the greasy hair atop his head. He was wearing a red sleeveless shirt with yellow words that read: "GOD IS LOVE". Their eyes locked, and the man waved a light, happy little wave.

"*What the fuck?*" Denny yelled, still half-stunned.

The man grinned. "This is your new home. You like it?"

Denny didn't understand, *couldn't* understand. He looked at the chains attached to the cuffs again, his eyes following them up the wall to the ceiling, where they were attached to some kind of screw hook. He looked at his feet, now seeing that they were also shackled, their chains leading to similar hooks in the wall.

In that moment, Allie's face appeared in his mind, and he became both frightened and enraged. He looked at the fat bastard, angry now. "*Where is she?*"

The man was visibly confused. "Who? Where is *who?*"

"*My granddaughter Allie!*"

His head cocked as he stared at Denny, trying to decipher his words.

"I don't understand," he said.

"You kidnapped her, you fat fuck!"

Realization washed over his face. His lips curled into a smile that was almost innocent but still completely terrifying. "Well, why didn't you say so?"

"Where is she?" Denny asked, hearing his voice wavering.

"Depends. Which one was she?"

Catching the implication, Denny's bravado dropped. "She's a redhead," he managed, feeling deflated.

The guy looked up, his face brightening. He raised his finger like he'd come up with an idea. "Sure, the redhead," he said, nodding. "That was a long time ago." He looked directly at Denny now. "How long ago was that?"

Denny's heart sunk further. There were tears welling up in his eyes, blinding him. He wanted to be angry, and he wanted to be violent, but all he could manage was overwhelming sadness. He felt broken. He looked at the man through tear-filled eyes. "It was 13... 13 years."

The man nodded. "Time sure flies, huh? Yeah. I remember her. McDonalds, right?"

Denny looked at him, killing him with his stare. The more he stared, the angrier he became, until he was completely overcome with rage. He bolted towards the man, trying to get on his feet, but he slipped, falling forward. When he did, he was suddenly stopped by the chains, yanking him back. He growled angrily, but his growl faded into a wail of despair akin to the yelp of a wounded animal. He stared at the man, screaming now, crying as he did, *"You better hope I don't get free, you motherfucker!"*

The man sat there, unmoved. "You won't," he said flatly. "No one ever does."

George Harrison was on the radio now, *Give Me Love* playing.

Denny stared at the guy, completely consumed by hate and

anger. Feeling hopeless, he resisted, wanting to lash out, but finding nothing he could do but spit at him. So he did. The spittle reached the man's face, becoming sparse because of the distance between them. The corners of his lips curled into a smile. He raised his hand, scooping up spittle from his beard and bringing it to his lips. He made eye contact with Denny, letting him see he wasn't intimidated. He licked his fingers.

As Denny watched, he now realized he was trembling and wondered if it was anger or fear, deciding both. No matter what, Denny wouldn't let this sonofabitch see how pained he was. Not anymore. Not again. Denny started to say something smart, but tried to reposition his feet as he did, stepping on something. Denny looked down, moving his foot back to see what it was. He squinted at it, craning down to see.

The man watched, waiting for a reaction. Denny squatted, reaching for it. As he grew closer to the floor, he saw what he'd stepped on – a bloody human finger. He looked up, seeing the man already laughing. Denny stared at the fucker, watching him laugh like he'd seen the funniest thing ever.

"*Jesus Christ!*" screamed Denny.

The man nodded. "Jesus Christ, indeed. You're a sinner, buddy. That's why I'm here. I'm gonna help you atone for your sins."

"How..." Denny began, pausing. "How do you know I'm a sinner? You don't know shit about me."

"Everyone's a sinner, my friend. *Everyone.* My job here is to make people see the error of their ways. My job is to make them... Sorry, make *YOU* atone for your sins."

"You're a fuckin' loon," said Denny. "Who are you to decide that?"

"I've been sent from God to make sinners suffer. That's my job."

Denny glared. "Who says?"

"God says," the man said, smiling proudly. "He came to me. In a dream. One night when I was about 20 or so. He said: 'Cordell, I've got a job for you. It's a tough job. Not everybody's cut out for it. But you are, Cordell. You are." Cordell looked at Denny, animated now, getting into it. "He says: 'I want you to make 'em pay. All of 'em. Make 'em pay.' I said: 'What do you mean, God?' And he says: 'You know what I mean.' Make the fuckers hurt. Make 'em bleed." Still staring at Denny, his head bounced giddily, almost a nod. "So that's what I do. I make 'em bleed."

"You're a fuckin' idiot," spat Denny.

Cordell nodded. "Maybe. But I'm the idiot who's in charge. And you and me, we're gonna have fun. Lots and lots of fun. So much fun you won't be able to stand it. You know why God picked me for this job? Do ya?"

Denny said nothing.

"He picked me because he saw something in me that he liked. Something special. You know what that was?"

"That you're a fuckhead?"

"No," said Cordell, grinning. "I like to hurt people. I like to hurt 'em real, *real* bad. I like to make 'em cry. I like to watch their expressions change as I do it."

"How do you do it?"

Cordell smiled wider. "You'll find out soon enough."

Despite already knowing he was in a terrible situation, Denny now felt truly frightened. It now occurred to him that he would never leave this basement alive. He looked at Cordell, sitting there grinning.

"What did you do with Baby Allie?"

Cordell stared into his eyes, not blinking. "You mean, what did I do *to* Baby Allie."

Denny was so engaged in the moment, so focused on the

asshole before him, that he wasn't even aware he was crying. Not until his breath caught as he heaved.

Denny wanted to say something tough, wanted to assert himself, but he couldn't. There was no point and he was tired. All he could manage was to look at the bastard, whimpering as he did.

"I did what I do," said Cordell, boasting. "I showed her that she was on the wrong path."

Denny screamed again. *"She was only seven! What the fuck kinda path should she have been on?"*

Cordell looked at him, trying to show compassion, trying to make him understand. "We all have our sins. Even her, fella. Even a seven-year-old. She did something wrong. Something. I don't know what. She probably did *lots* of things."

"No, no she didn't."

"She did. I assure you, she did. Why else would God have sent me?"

"God didn't send shit!" screamed Denny. *"No one sent you, you piece of shit!"*

"You're wrong," said Cordell, still calm, sounding cool, almost monotone. He pointed towards the ceiling. "*He* sent me. God sent me to punish that little bitch, just like he sent me to punish you. It's all part of his divine plan." He looked at Denny. "What's your name?"

"Fuck you," growled Denny. "That's my name."

Cordell smiled, nodding animatedly, like a silent chuckle. "Alrighty then," he said. "I don't need to know your name. Don't care. God knows your name. That's all that matters. And he brought you here to me so I could teach you. So I could make you bleed. And best be sure, bleed is what you're gonna do."

Denny sat there in silence, trying to figure out a move.

Cordell continued. "You've been bad, buddy. That's all

there is to it. You been bad and I gotta correct that. I gotta show you the way."

"And what's the way?"

Cordell looked at him like he was stupid. "God, obviously. God is the way. God is *always* the way. Don't you know that?"

Denny looked down, kicking the severed finger angrily. He looked up at Cordell. "So, you're telling me Allie is dead?"

Cordell sighed. "Apparently I'm not getting through to you. Yes, the little cunt is gone. She's been worm food for, what did you say, 13 years? I couldn't keep her alive. I had no choice. I had to teach her a lesson and get her outta here to make room for the next motherfucker God sends. You know, the next person who needed punished."

"In God's name?"

Cordell nodded, staring into his eyes. He did it nonchalantly. "You betcha. Everything is for him."

Denny's energy surged and he bolted towards Cordell again, his arms reaching out. *"You motherfu..!"* He reached the end of the chain again, jarring him. He recoiled, as if in shock. He looked at the cement floor. Now he saw the piles of dried shit piled around him along the wall. He turned towards Cordell. "Is this shit?"

Cordell grinned. "It ain't blueberry pie."

"Why?"

"Why you think? Where else do you think you're gonna shit and piss? This is your home, Barney. You better get used to it."

Denny looked at him, trying to understand. "Why did you call me Barney?"

"Cause that's your new name. Barney. I just decided. So it is written, so it shall be done. And your ass is Barney."

Denny tried to twist his face into the most sarcastic expression he could manage, but didn't know if he pulled it off. "You're a real piece of work, you know that?"

"I do," said Cordell proudly. "I know because God tells me. He loves the work I do. He appreciates it. He says I'm the very best at what I do." He looked at Denny, his expression changing, and his voice became quieter, more solemn. "There are others like me, Barney. Lots of others. But God says that of all those people, I'm the best."

Denny resigned himself to the situation and sat down, thinking he would find a solution along the way.

Cordell sat there across from him, smiling. "It's time, Barney."

"For what?"

Cordell smiled, reaching behind him, but Denny couldn't see what he was reaching for. Then he produced an object that looked like a piece of pipe. Except it was made of wood. Denny thought it was a flute at first, thought the asshole was gonna play him a tune.

Cordell raised it to his lips, but then raised its barrel towards Denny. Before it registered what was happening, Denny heard the *pffffft!* sound and felt the sting of the dart sticking him in the belly. Denny looked down, stunned, seeing it there. He reached for it, grabbing it, and pulled it out. Stunned, he looked at his captor.

Cordell winked. "You ready to rock 'n' roll?"

SEVEN

DENNY COULD HEAR *Delta Dawn* before he even opened his eyes. The first thing that struck him on waking was that his head now hurt even worse than before. The second realization was that he was lying on a table, strapped down, in a different room. He could move his head a little, leaning it forward, getting a glimpse of the straps across his arms and torso, and also his midsection, just above his flaccid penis. He couldn't see the straps on his legs, but he could feel them. He tried to move them, testing the straps, finding them tight. He moved his head to the side, seeing Cordell standing there, looking down at him.

"Howdy, Barn," he said. "You sleep well?"

Denny didn't say anything, still trying to figure it all out.

"Do you like my blowgun? It's just like the ones aborigines use. I saw it on an old episode of *Gilligan's Island* and I knew I had to have it. So I made it. That's really how it is, isn't it? If you want something, you just gotta do it yourself. They don't got aborigine blowguns at Walmart."

Denny strained his neck to look at him, but his vision was blurry. "What did you shoot me with? Some kinda poison?"

"Just a little something to knock you out," said Cordell. "It's safe." Cordell paused for a moment and then laughed at what he'd said. "*It's safe!* Like *that's* the part you gotta worry about. No, that's the safe part, Barney. I made the concoction myself. Looked it up on the internet. Just somethin' to render you unconscious for a bit so I can do what I needa do without you fuckin' around and interfering."

Denny looked at him through blurred eyes. "What did you do to me?"

Cordell laughed again. "What? You think I raped you while you were out? Maybe played with your balls a little? No, nothing like that. That would be untoward. This is God's work, Barney. I'm not here to play with your balls. I'm here to hurt you. Hurt you bad. Make you bleed and scream. Until..."

The words hung there for a moment.

"Until what?" asked Denny.

"Until you can't scream anymore."

"What does that mean?"

Cordell chuckled. He reached up and flicked his index finger against Denny's forehead, popping him. "Not too bright, are ya, Barn? Until you're dead, obviously."

Denny didn't react. He'd been terrified this entire time, so there was no escalation. Looking at Cordell, he asked: "What did you do to Allie?" As the words left Denny's lips, he felt himself on the verge of tears again. "What did you do, you bastard?"

"I'm sure you think I'm some kinda monster."

"You're worse than a monster," Denny blurted, louder than a statement but quieter than a yell.

Cordell said, "I did the same thing to her I'm gonna do to you. I played *the game.*"

Denny's neck was hurting now from twisting it to his left

for so long, but he held his eyes on the fat piece of shit. "What game?"

"*THE* game. God's game. I call it that because I don't know what else to call it. God told me about it, told me how to play it, but he didn't give me a name for it. But the game... That's what we're gonna play, you and me. I play it with everyone who comes down here."

Denny was whimpering, but not wanting to.

"Does anybody ever survive?" asked Denny.

"Yeah. I do. But nobody else."

"How many people have there been?"

Cordell's face contorted as he considered this. "I dunno," he said. "Maybe 30, 40. Something like that. I lost track after the first 12 or so. After my granddaddy. He was the first really significant one. Other than the first, of course. The first is always significant, even if it ain't. Like, you know, when you lost your virginity." Cordell stared off in silence for a moment before turning back to him. "Funny thing is, my first murder was the same person I lost my virginity to. My daddy."

"*You killed your daddy?*" And then, a couple seconds later, "And your daddy *fucked* you?"

"Daddy was terrible, so I had to do it. I... I had ta kill him. But I didn't play the game with him, really. I didn't know the rules yet. I just stuck a knife in his face. Then I took him out back of my uncle's place and buried him real deep so no one would find the miserable old fuck. Nobody ever did either, and that's when I knew I was special. Then, just a few months later, God came to me in a dream and confirmed it. That's when he told me that I had to make people suffer. So that's what I been doin' ever since. It's hard work, but it's the Lord's work."

Denny glared at him. "You like what you do."

Cordell's face brightened and he stiffened a bit, leaning back. "Shit yes, I do. Everybody's good at something. Writers are good at writing, Donnie Trump is good at presidenting... We all got somethin', Barn. All of us. Some people are good at things they don't particularly like doing." Cordell smiled, looking proud of himself. He tapped his chest. "But not me. Not me, Barn. Not at all. My work is my pleasure. That's why the big guy chose me. He knew. He knew it before I did. I'm special."

"You're a fuck." In the background, Denny could hear Lobos' *I'd Love You To Want Me* playing.

Cordell nodded. "That's your opinion. Not mine. Not God's. To us, *you're* the fuck, Barney. That's why you're here. That's why he brought you and your little cunt kid to me."

Before Cordell could say anything more, Denny bucked, trying to break free of his straps, but managed nothing. Cordell just laughed, flicking him in the forehead with his finger again.

"You poor dumb bastard," he said. "You really are pitiful. Now I understand."

"What? What do you understand?"

Cordell looked upon him like he was something to be pitied. "I understand why the Lord brought you. You're a bad man, Barn. *Real* bad."

Denny glared. "Says the guy who keeps people in his basement and murders them."

"What I do ain't murder, Barn. Not really. I know that sounds like semantics, but this is something different, something more. So much more. This is important work, what I do. Like I said, this is God's work."

Denny spit at him again. Cordell turned his head, letting the spittle hit him in the side of his face. He wiped it off with the back of his hand.

"We gotta play the game now. We've spent enough time fuckin' around."

Here it came, Denny thought. But what was it? He didn't

know anything beyond the fact that it scared the hell out of him.

"What is this game? What are the rules?"

Cordell smiled with devilish delight. "Here's the rules, Barn. Every day you're here, I cut off a part of your body."

Denny felt sick to his stomach. He wanted to scream at him, wanted to plead and fight, but he knew it was no use. He remained calm, trying to let the words sink in.

"Every day," said Cordell. "One day it might be a finger, the next your dick."

My dick? This frightened Denny and he could feel a tingle in his dick, as if mentioning it had somehow brought it to life.

"Oh yeah, your dick. That's the best part. That's why I really prefer men over women. I mean, there's things that I can do with a woman that I can't do with a man. After all, I'm not queer or anything. I'm not like Daddy. I don't play with people's cocks."

"You just cut 'em off."

Cordell nodded matter-of-factly. "Right. I just cut 'em off. But not right away. I like to stretch it out. The key is, you can't wait too long or the guy dies before you get to cut off his dick. I mean, everyone dies here, right? But I like to make it last. I've found if I do it right, if I cut off fingers and toes and ears first, maybe poke out an eye, the guy lives longer. This shit is too much work to waste those opportunities. I wanna get the most bang for my buck I can, Barn. I wanna stretch it out and make it last."

Denny felt sick to his stomach. "How long do people usually survive this game?"

"Depends. I had one gal, good-lookin' gal..." He looked up to make eye contact with Denny again, a sick grin on his face. "We did some stuff. Sex stuff. I won't even tell you about it.

Good pussy though. Anyway, she died real quick. She did something that pissed me off, forced me to kill her the second day. She was one of the first ones, so I didn't really know what I was doin' yet, you know? But she forced me to do it."

"What did she do?"

Cordell looked at him, a sour expression on his face. "She hurt me. Hurt me *real bad*. With her mouth."

Denny grinned. "She bite your dick off?"

"No. Thankfully not. She just chewed one of my balls off. So you see, I had no choice. I had to kill that bitch. I didn't deserve that kinda shit. I'm a good guy, Barney. I wasn't tryin' to be mean or anything like that. That's not my way. I'm a good guy. A servant of God, doing the Lord's work. But you know how it is. Servants of God are always persecuted. You look in your Bible, Barn, you'll see it always happens that way. It's been happening since the beginning of time."

"You and me, I don't think we follow the same God."

Cordell nodded. "I think you're right. I do. I think that's why you're here." Cordell pointed at the ceiling. "He knows what he's doin', Barn. He *always* knows. And he brought you here, so there musta been a reason. You been bad. Somehow, some way, you been bad. But I'm here to take care of that."

"By cutting off my fingers?"

Cordell's eyes got big. "Oh yes, Barn. Most definitely. By cutting off everything I can before you die. You know how long the guy who lived the longest lasted?"

Denny stared at him, waiting.

"Not gonna answer?" asked Cordell. "Doesn't matter. The guy, an old hillbilly dude, looked like a lumberjack, probably fucked farm animals, he lived two-and-a-half weeks. It was impressive. But I made a few mistakes along the way. For instance, I messed up and poked out both his eyes the first week. That was dumb. I didn't know it then, but it was. You know what I learned, Barn?"

Denny stared at him, not speaking.

Cordell sighed and flicked him in the temple again.

"You flick me again and I'll kill you," said Denny.

Cordell ignored it. "I found out if you poke out a person's eyes, it's not all that fun anymore. It ain't fun if they can't watch you. That's so much more rewarding." Cordell stood in silence, looking off. Then he turned back to Denny. "This is hard work, Barn. I deserve to be compensated for what I do. And I am. You know how? God allows me the satisfaction of being able to fully enjoy what I do. And that means stretching it out and making it as enjoyable as I can." He smiled. "Enjoyable for *me*. Not for you. You ain't gonna enjoy it. But you know what I mean. It's more fun to have them watch me while I cut off parts of their bodies. So that's what I do. And God lets me have my fun as long as I'm doing his work."

"Like raping women?"

Cordell nodded. "Perks of the job."

"Did you rape Allie?"

Denny regretted asking the question the moment the words left his lips.

Cordell lit up, beaming. "Oh yes, Barn. I *loved* it. Absolutely *loved* it. And she did, too. She was *so* good. The best. Just the best."

"FUCKER!" screamed Denny, surging forward, trying to break his bonds again, to no avail.

"This kinda behavior is why you're here. So anyway, that's what the game is. Those are the rules. You ready to play?"

EIGHT

Cordell stood there grinning like a fool with his hands behind his back. "Guess what I got?" he asked. "A gift. For you." Denny watched, wondering what it would be, knowing it wouldn't be anything good. Cordell started to move his right arm and his hand came out from behind him. Denny looked and could see what it was, even before Cordell held it out in front of him. It was a steak knife. Nothing particularly menacing, but it was frightening enough since Denny knew Cordell was going to use it to hurt him.

"You like steak, Barn?" asked Cordell. He paused for a moment, staring at Denny excitedly, and then began giggling like a schoolgirl. "Sure you do. Everyone likes steak. But this, this is gonna be different. You're gonna be the steak, Barney. How many people ever get to say that in their lifetime?"

Denny felt angry but deflated. Instead of fighting against the straps, he tried to reason with Cordell. "You don't need to do this. We can talk about it. Maybe we can work something out."

Cordell grinned. "That's cute. Really it is."

"I've got money. I can pay you."

Cordell was unmoved. "That's what they all say. All of 'em. Even your whore granddaughter. She was little, but she still knew enough to say that her grandpa would pay to save her." He looked into Denny's eyes. "Was that you? Were you the grandpa she thought would come and save her?"

Denny glared at him. "Fuck you."

"You never came, Barney. You never came to save her. That little bitch cried and cried, waiting for someone to come and save her. But no one ever did." He paused, his eyes locked with Denny's. "*YOU* never came."

Denny could feel the tears welling up in his eyes again, but he said nothing. Meat Loaf's *Two Out of Three Ain't Bad* was playing in the background. There seemed always to be seventies soft rock playing.

"She waited and waited, Barn, until finally..."

"What?"

Cordell turned his head, looking at him with pity. "You know what I did. I did what I'm gonna do to you. She played the game. *We* played the game, the two of us."

"And she lost," Denny said sickly.

"Everyone loses. Just the way it is. It's a rigged game, Barney. But don't look at me. I'm not that kinda guy. I would never rig a game. It was him." Cordell pointed up again. "God rigged it. Thing is, even though we call it a game, it ain't no game at all. It's you paying penance for your misdeeds."

"And Allie paid a penance?"

Cordell nodded. "Sure she did. That's how it goes. And I sawed her up. Cut her. I can't remember. I do it different every time. The key is to keep it fresh. It's like your sex life; you gotta keep it spiced up or it gets boring after a while. I never woulda thought it, but killin' folks gets tiresome. Once you've done it as many times as I have, there's nothing new. I've heard every scream and moan and cry there is to hear. I've heard skin slice and dice and tear and I've heard the bones snap and shatter. I've heard it all. So I can't say as I recall the exact events of the little whore's death, but they're all pretty much the same. The end result is the same."

Cordell stood there for a moment, Denny staring at him, both of them thinking. Then Cordell looked up again. "There was one difference though," he said. "Her death was different than yours is gonna be. Back then, I used to eat the people."

Denny looked at him, wanting to scream and fight and buck but without the strength to do so. Instead he just said weakly, "You...*ate*...her?"

Cordell nodded. "'Fraid so. Back then I ate 'em all. I was a bit of a caveman, I guess. I'm not proud of it. None of it really. The taste wasn't so hot either. Lots of gristle. I would eat 'em though, figurin' it was a good way to dispose of those bodies. But if you don't eat 'em fast, they start to rot. And I don't have a freezer. I thought about..."

Denny found a surge of renewed strength and bucked again, trying to sit forward but wasn't able to move inside his straps. His head was still turned even though his neck hurt like hell, and he stared at Cordell. *"You piece of filth!"*

Cordell looked sad now. "I know you feel that way, Barn, but you gotta look at it from my perspective. Imagine God came to you and asked you to do something..."

"Fuck you," growled Denny.

Cordell ignored this. "What would you do? You'd do it, right? You'd have to. After all, he created us. Both of us, me and you. The little redhead, too. He created all of us. So if he asks me to do somethin', I'm gonna do it. And he told me to cut you guys up, so that's what I do."

Denny was trembling with anger. "He didn't tell you to eat them."

Cordell grinned. "He didn't say not to either."

All of this was ridiculous, Denny thought. God hadn't told him to do anything. None of it. This fucker was nuts, plain and simple.

Cordell leaned in. His empty hand came up from the side of the table and grabbed Denny's strapped-down wrist, then sliding his hand over the back of Denny's. When Denny felt Cordell's hand, he jerked, bucking again, but accomplished nothing.

"No need to fight," said Cordell. "You can't stop this. No one has ever been able to stop it. I figure at the end of the day it's better to just go with it and let it happen. It's easier on every-body that way."

"Fuck!" Denny screamed, angry at his own helplessness.

Cordell's hand slid along Denny's to his pinky. He reached under the finger and seized it. Although Denny could still wiggle his fingers, he found that he could do nothing to fight him off. Cordell gripped the pinky.

"You ready to play the game, Barn?"

Denny shook in the straps, trying to wriggle, moving his fingers.

"Please stop," said Cordell.

Denny continued moving his hands, trying to accomplish something. Anything.

"I said stop!"

Denny kept wiggling his fingers.

Cordell angrily bent Denny's pinky all the way back, snap-ping the bone.

A surge of sharp pain unlike anything Denny had ever known shot through his finger. His stomach felt sour and he screamed in agony.

"I told you to stop," Cordell said. "You gotta learn to listen."

Denny wanted to tell him to go fuck himself, but he was in too much pain to focus on anything else.

"That was just the beginning," said Cordell.

Cordell's right hand came up from beneath the table. The hand with the knife. He took it and pressed its blade against the top of the broken finger, which he still held with his other hand.

Despite the pain, Denny managed, *"Please, no. Please."*

But Cordell was looking down, focusing on the task at hand. Denny could feel the blade pressing against the pinky.

Cordell looked up. "There's different ways to do this. I could just sort of push down real hard and cut it mostly off all at once." He smiled at Denny. "But I ain't gonna do that. No, no. That's not the way we do things here. You know how I do it?"

Denny stared at him though tears, half in shock, saying nothing.

"I do it the slow-as-fuck painful-as-all-hell way. I don't even slice the way you slice meat. No, no. That's too quick. Instead I saw at it, just a little at a time. I drag it out and make it last. More fun that way."

Denny couldn't see the hand from the angle where his head was strapped down, but he could feel that blade. And then it started moving, back and forth, back and forth, pressing only a bit.

"No, please," begged Denny.

Cordell said nothing, just kept sawing. It started to hurt almost at once, a little at first and then building into sharp, excruciating pain.

Denny screamed. *"Please, no, please stop! I'll do anything!"*

Cordell looked up at him, the blade still sawing through the finger. "You'll die is what you'll do." He was still looking at him, smiling gleefully, when the blade reached the bone. "Ah, we've struck buried treasure," said Cordell gleefully. "Just gotta saw a little harder." He went back to sawing, applying lots of pressure, and Denny could hear the blade sawing through the bone. It hurt so much it took his breath away. He cried, moaned, bucked, and begged, but Cordell just kept sawing.

"How does that feel, Barn?" This was the last thing Denny heard before he passed out.

When he opened his eyes again a few minutes later, the pain was as intense as anything he'd ever known. So intense it made his stomach hurt terribly. Cordell was standing there looking at him, no longer sawing. Denny turned his eyes down his body, trying to see his hand but couldn't.

"Is it...*still there?*" he asked.

Cordell smiled. "No, no, of course not." Then he held up the severed pinky, holding it between his index finger and thumb. "It's right here, sport."

Denny bucked, trying to fight, his hand still hurting tremendously. *"YOU MOTHERFUCKER!"*

Cordell kept smiling. "That's not very nice, you know. You're not being a good sport about this at all. Back when I was a teacher I woulda given you a 'Doesn't Play Well with Others' on your report card. I know what you're thinking: 'This guy was a teacher?' But yes, I was a teacher."

Cordell was wrong; Denny wasn't thinking anything, couldn't give a shit less about what the fucker did or had done for a living. All he could think about was the pain, the horrible, excruciating pain.

"I was a damn good teacher, Barn," Cordell said. "One time I got a Teacher of the Year award. It wasn't the national one, though. It was just a regional one. But I was still proud of it. And believe it or not, I didn't kill the kids." He paused and then looked back at Denny. "Not *really* anyway. Just one."

Suddenly Denny was overcome with anger again. *"FUCK YOU!"*

"Tsk-tsk," said Cordell. "Your behavior is rather unbecoming." He looked down at Denny's hand. "We need to stop the bleeding. If we don't, you'll bleed out. Then the game would be over. I don't want that." He looked at Denny again. "Neither of us do. So we gotta take care of that."

Denny lay there in pain, looking up now, feeling the warm tears streaming down the sides of his temples. He hated this man, hated this place, but saw no way out. His hand hurt so incredibly badly he could hardly stand it. He felt proud for the briefest of moments that he was no longer screaming, but his breathing was heavy and his stomach hurt almost as much as his hand.

"This is how we stop the bleeding," said Cordell. Denny turned his head to see him standing there holding up a little handheld device that looked like some sort of *Star Wars* ray gun. "You ever see one of these before? This is what they call a culinary blowtorch."

BLOWTORCH? JESUS CHRIST, thought Denny.

"*No, no,*" he said, starting to cry harder. He just wanted it all to end. It had only been the one finger at this point, and he was already ready to die. He turned his head, looking at the ceiling, looking for God. He did this for a moment, silently praying for help. Then he heard the click. He turned his head and saw a thin blue flame emitting from the end of the blowtorch. Cordell leaned in towards the wounded hand.

"I gotta warn you, this is gonna hurt a bit," he said.

"*No, please, no.*"

Denny felt immense heat right in the center of the already-existing pain. Suddenly the pain was masked, obscured by the even worse searing heat. Denny screamed out, feeling his bladder release and he pissed himself. He felt the urine but couldn't focus on it. All he could manage to focus on was the extreme heat, which seemed to reach through the rest of his hand and radiate up his arm.

"You should see this," said Cordell. "It's really cool. The skin just sort of melts together in a big blob."

Denny continued to scream.

NINE

When Denny started to wake up, he was lying naked on the cement floor again, chained to the wall. Tony Orlando and Dawn were singing *Knock Three Times*, and the stump where Denny's pinky had been hurt beyond belief. He heard himself moaning over the song as his eyes fluttered open and closed. Once he'd become accustomed to the overhead light, he sat up, his tailbone hurting pressed against the cold, hard floor. He raised his hand to examine the pinky stump. *Jesus Christ*, he thought. It was grotesque. Just as Cordell had described it, there was a mushy-looking glob of skin – now solidified – atop the stump. His hand was dirty, dirt in every fingernail and crack, and there was dried blood covering it.

His head hurt, his stomach hurt, and most of all the stump hurt. He sat there, feeling sick, and looked around the room. The walls were all gray cement. There was no furniture. Just the old boombox radio sitting on the floor in the corner, playing all the seventies songs. Denny looked down at his flaccid penis, making sure it was still intact. Discovering that it was, he went about looking over his body, but found nothing unexpected. He then raised his wrists, examining the steel cuffs that bound them. He moved them around and tugged on them, turning them over, and eventually concluded they were as secure as Cordell had said they were. Next, he examined the chains, his eyes following them up the wall and to the ceiling. He could see no way out. Then he looked up at the overhead light, hanging from the ceiling. It was a primitive thing, and Denny realized he could jump for it and likely strike it, breaking it. But what good would that do? None. It would only make this bad situation a hundred times worse. The life he was now living was about as bad a thing as he could imagine, but he thought it would be even worse in darkness.

Thankfully the room was fairly warm. He was a man prone to becoming cold easily. His doctor had said it was poor circulation. But it wasn't cold in here, which was a plus. His situation could have been better, but being warm was a small nicety. Sitting there, he looked over towards the wall he was attached to. He looked first at the large piles of dried shit along the side, thinking it was good to pile it in one place so as to leave room for unencumbered movement. Then he looked at the dried blood stains. Many of them were dark and stood out. But, on closer inspection, he now saw there were older, faded blood stains around and beneath them, almost invisible at first glance. This led him to conclude that Cordell had been truthful about the number of people he'd kept and killed. Looking along the wall, he noticed a blackened, severed hand lying in the corner, out of his reach. He wasn't even startled anymore. *Damn*, he thought, considering the poor bastard who'd lost it. But then, he realized, a hand was nothing compared to everything else that had been lost here.

This led his mind back to Allie, the reason he'd come here in the first place. Could she really be dead? Was Cordell telling him the truth? He tried to make himself believe otherwise, tried to grasp on to an explanation as to how or why she might have escaped and could still be alive, but he inevitably settled on the likely truth – she was dead and had been for more than a decade. Maybe even eaten. This thought sickened him and he tried to push it from his mind.

Making this worse, Cordell had been correct; Denny hadn't come for her. He hadn't saved her. He'd done everything he possibly could have done – *he had, hadn't he?* – but that didn't change the reality that Baby Allie had sat down here, enduring God knows what, frightened and alone, waiting for her Denny-Pa to show up and save her. But he hadn't. And thinking about it now, he came to the conclusion that, at the age of seven, she wouldn't have understood why he hadn't come. The likely reality was that she sat down here, being cut apart and tortured, maybe even raped along the way, thinking her Denny-Pa had forgotten her.

He started to cry. He had always been a sadomasochist in this way, inflicting pain upon himself and dwelling on the elements of his family members' deaths that would hurt him most. Sitting here now, naked and dirty and without a finger, tears streaming down his face, he wondered why he'd never killed himself. And he hated himself for not doing it. Had he done it, he would never have known the awful truth about Baby Allie. But no, that would have been the easy way out, just as he'd always believed. Because if he had grown a pair and had actually taken his own life, he would have spared himself this pain – pain he deserved. He deserved it for all the things he had done wrong, from his lackadaisical approach to his wife and family to his leaving Baby Allie alone to be kidnapped. He'd always been a failure. A failure at everything. Well, he thought again, except for being a cop.

But even that was a lie, wasn't it? His mind went back to memories he'd suppressed for so long. Thoughts about dirty money he'd taken from criminals, drugs and money he'd stolen from those he'd apprehended, and the suspects he'd hurt without justification. Sure, every cop he knew was doing those things, but it wasn't right. It had been wrong, just like everything else he'd ever done in his life.

Shitty husband, shitty father, shitty grandfather, shitty cop. Thinking about it now, he saw it all more clearly than he ever had before. Perhaps it was the pain, he thought. Maybe something about the tremendous pain throbbing in his hand was sharpening his thought processes, making him see things more clearly. Or maybe the opposite was true. Maybe the pain was making him see these things wrong. Maybe he wasn't so bad. But he knew in his heart this was a lie. He was bad and had always been bad. He'd built a life on taking shortcuts and looking out for number one. Always.

But... No, that wasn't the truth. Not with Allie. He remembered now how he'd seen Allie as his shot at redemption. Sure, he'd failed her, but he'd legitimately tried. His best hadn't been good enough – it never had – but by God he'd tried to be a good parent, for lack of another word. He'd been Allie's Denny-Pa, her stand-in parent, her protector.

He thought about that. *Her protector.* That hadn't worked out so well, had it?

He sat there on the cold floor, crying, his balls on the cement. As he did, he saw a cockroach scurry across in front of him. When he saw it, he suddenly knew a hard truth. Not in his mind, but in his being. In every part of him. If he was to survive, he would have to eat whatever he was presented with. Things like this cockroach. Before the thought fully registered, some long-dormant animal instinct made him roll forward and lunge, chains jangling, towards the cockroach. It scurried and he thought it might escape, but he stopped it with his left hand, scooping it into his right. He clasped his hands together, sandwiching the insect. He raised his shackled hands before his face, staring at them. He suddenly felt sick, but also felt hungry.

Fuck it, he thought. He had to do whatever it took.

He raised his closed hands to his mouth, squeezed them open a bit, and forced the insect between his lips. When it first entered his mouth, he felt its legs trying to run, but he bit down hard, feeling it squish in his teeth. He tried to chew fast and swallow the thing before it could move any further and before he could fully taste it. Despite this, he still tasted it. It was a rich, strange taste. It was mostly texture, and that texture disgusted him. He finished chewing and swallowed it, feeling his stomach buckle as he did. Once he'd downed it, he sat there feeling gross.

How long had he been here? He couldn't be sure, but he thought it had been less than a day.

All By Myself was playing on the radio now. The song momentarily took him back to his childhood. He had been very young when the song came out, but he remembered hearing it once in a specific memory that seemed remarkably unspectacular, so he wondered why he remembered it. He was sitting in his parents' car and the song was playing on one of his Dad's eight-tracks. His Dad had a lot of eight-tracks back then. Denny was gone, out of this basement, for a moment, remembering those eight-tracks. He remembered seeing Queen's *News of the World* album in his Dad's collection. Years later, when Denny had gotten older and had come to love Queen, he had remembered this. When he asked his Dad about it, now believing his Dad had been cooler than he'd given him credit for, his Dad had quickly dashed away this idea by telling him that God no, he would have never listened to Queen and that it had simply come in the mail as a result of his not having sent in his monthly Columbia House Record Club form.

Denny thought about that, a smile on his face, and then snapped back to the present. He blinked, looking around the room, finding it to be just as hopeless as he had thought it previously. Sitting there, waiting for Cordell to return to torture him further, Denny felt his stomach move and realized he needed to shit. The thought of this terrified him. Certainly taking a shit naked and chained up in a stranger's basement wasn't as frightening as having just had his finger sawed off, but it still wasn't pleasant. He thought about it for a moment, trying to build up his will to do it, when his stomach churned again, forcing the issue. Denny didn't want to do it, but he crawled towards the piles of shit along the wall. When he got about a foot from them, he lifted himself up on squatting legs and turned, his back towards the wall. He looked up at the top of the stairs. He watched as he began moving his bowels. Cordell did not emerge from the door, but somehow focusing on that made all this the tiniest bit easier. As he finished the deed, it occurred to Denny that there was no toilet paper here. He then considered all this entailed. Feeling sick about it, he moved himself forward, away from the wall, and sat, already feeling his ass itching.

Denny sat there for a long time, lost in his thoughts. Finally, after a long while, he lay down on the cement floor. The floor hurt and it was difficult to find comfort, especially with the chains attached to him, but eventually he drifted off to sleep.

Some time later – Denny had no idea how long it was – he was awakened by the sound of the door atop the stairs. He looked up, seeing it was open. Cordell was in the doorway, starting to make his way down. Denny watched him. Cordell was carrying a large yellow bag. At first Denny didn't know what it was, but as Cordell came closer, Denny realized it was dry dog food. Maybe he should have been angry or upset by this, but he wasn't. He was actually pleased by the prospect of being able to eat more than cockroaches. As he thought about this, it also registered that eating the dog food would only prolong all this, but it was human nature. Denny didn't want to die. Even though he knew it would inevitably occur, he wanted to put it off for as long as possible. And maybe subsisting on dog food would keep him alive long enough to figure out a way to escape.

When Cordell reached the base of the stairs, he moved towards Denny, who was sitting up now. When he was just out of Denny's reach, Cordell stuck his hand into the bag. Denny could hear the dog food shifting around in there. Then Cordell's hand came up with a cup of dog food.

"This'll keep you alive for the moment," Cordell said.

He slung the dog food from the cup at Denny, and it slid across the floor towards him. Denny looked down at it, feeling strangely hungry for only having been here a day or so.

"*Bon appetit*," said Cordell. "Don't eat too fast. It's all you get until tomorrow."

Seeing Cordell making his way back up the steps with the bag, Denny leaned forward and started scooping up the pieces of dog food, stuffing them into his mouth.

TEN

When Denny woke up, the side of his head hurt where it had been lying against the cement. He squinted, focusing first on the pain. It was only after a second or two that he remembered where he was and what had happened. Almost on cue, likely psychosomatic, his hand started to hurt. Or, more likely, he thought, it had been hurting all along but he hadn't noticed it – perhaps used to it by now – until he remembered his finger being cut off.

He sat up, his neck hurting. He was facing the wall he was chained to. He pulled himself up further, sitting upright now, his chains jingling as he moved. He shook his head, trying to clear his head.

That was when he heard Cordell's voice from behind him. "Oh, good. You're awake, Barn."

The voice startled him. It also frightened him, a fact which sickened him. Even in his current flabby, broken-down state, Denny could have beat the living shit out of Cordell quite easily on the outside in a normal confrontation. But this was not that. This was Cordell's basement, where Cordell was god. Quite simply, this was hell.

Denny turned his body, sitting with his legs crossed, to face his captor, also sitting on the floor. Cordell was grinning. The grin looked sadistic, but Denny figured it was probably the same grin the fucker had always had and that it just seemed sadistic now since Denny knew what he was capable of. Denny hated that he was afraid of the sonofabitch, but he couldn't help it. The fucker had taken his finger.

Denny looked him in his eyes. "What now, dickhead? We gonna play another stupid-ass game?"

Cordell shrugged. "Yes and no."

Denny looked at him, trying to decipher this.

"We're gonna play a game, yes. Most certainly. But it won't be *another* game. No, no, Barney. This is gonna be the *same* game. But I like you. You inspire me." He stared at Denny, waiting for a reaction. "What do you think about that?"

"I don't give a shit what you think."

Cordell shook his head as if he was dealing with a disobedient child. "Not nice, Barn. Not nice at all. But you inspire me. You really do. There's something different about you. Not different in that you'll survive or any silly thing like that, but something more interesting than the usual."

Denny gave him a strange look, trying to understand.

"I can't quite put my finger on it," said Cordell. He made a face, grinned wider, and looked back up at Denny. "Maybe I can. Maybe I can put *your* finger on it! What do you think of that?"

"Fuck you," growled Denny. When he saw Cordell's grin spread, he spat at him again, his spittle falling short.

"I know, not a good joke. But you can't blame a guy for trying. Funny thing, but I wanted to be a comedian once upon a time a long time ago. Back before I was a teacher."

Denny couldn't believe Cordell had been a teacher. Thinking of him spending time around children repulsed him. Then his mind went back to Allie. Before he could mention her, Cordell spoke again. "There's something about you that's different. It makes me want to do something completely different to you. Different from the things I've done to all the others. Something unique."

"Here's an idea," said Denny. "Why don't you eat shit and die?" The way he said it, it was more a statement than a question.

Cordell ignored this, as he was prone to. "I'm gonna hurt you in a whole different way, Barn. I'm gonna really fuck you up. I wanna make you suffer. I think it's the least I can do, really."

He sat there grinning, maybe trying to provoke Denny. If he was, it was working. Denny didn't want to be affected by the goofy bastard, but he was. Oh, yes, he most certainly was. He wanted so badly to tear the motherfucker to shreds. He briefly considered lunging at Cordell again, but he knew the chains would stop him, jerking him back. No, not today, thought Denny. Today he would just sit there and be calm and play the fucker's game. Maybe, just maybe, he thought, an opportunity would arise that would allow him to gain the upper hand.

Instead of attacking, Denny said, "I'm gonna get free. And when I do, I'm gonna hurt you real, real bad. I'm gonna do shit to you that's 10 times worse than the shit you've done to these people."

Cordell smiled. "No, you won't. It's a nice thought, fun to consider, but it's a fantasy. It's never happened before, and you won't be the first. God would never allow it. But I'm gonna hurt you something awful today."

Denny sat there trying to act tough, but he felt sick inside.

He had no idea what Cordell had in store for him, and it frightened him to consider it. It wouldn't be good, whatever it was.

Cordell said: "You like history, Barn?"

Denny scowled. "What the hell kinda question is that?"

"I like history. I used to teach history. Bet you didn't know that, did you?"

"Eat shit."

Cordell nodded. "Exactly the kind of statement I would expect from someone like you. Someone of your limited mentality."

This hit a nerve and Denny blurted: *"I'm smart, you dumb fuck!"* When he said it, he realized "I'm smart" wasn't the most intelligent thing to say, but it was what came to him in the moment. "I'm much smarter than you, you stupid piece of shit."

Cordell chuckled. "You think so? Then why is it you're the one in chains shitting in the corner and losing digits while I'm the one sitting here controlling your life?"

Denny stared at him, wanting to look tough, but instead looking pathetic. He had no answer.

"But history, Barn. Do you like it?"

"I guess," said Denny, relenting. "It's okay."

"You don't sound too sure."

Irritated, Denny asked, "What's your point?"

"My point is that we can learn a lot from history. Like the saying about us being doomed to repeat our mistakes if we don't learn from it."

"Is that what's gonna happen?" asked Denny. "You gonna teach me?"

"No, nothing like that," said Cordell, grinning big. "I'm just gonna hurt you. No teaching today. No, it was me who learned something from history. I find when I read books about history I learn new stuff all the time."

"You should learn to brush your yellow-ass teeth. You look like a fuckin' inbred."

"You wanna know what I'm reading about right now, Barn?"

"Not particularly."

"I'm reading a book about Native Americans. Do you know much about Native Americans?"

This irritated Denny. He was in no hurry to be hurt, but being hurt was far more enjoyable than listening to this asshole talk. Cordell was one of those guys who really enjoyed hearing himself speak. He hated the guy. Absolutely loathed him. He was someone he would have hated even if he hadn't done all the shit he'd done. If Denny had crossed paths with him back when he was a cop, well, things would have been different. The thought of this pleased Denny, thinking Cordell would have lost a few of those ugly yellow teeth.

When Denny didn't answer, Cordell continued. "I just read about the Blackfeet Indians. Do you know much about them?" Cordell paused for a moment, looking at him, obviously having already concluded he didn't. "Reading about the Blackfeet Indians intrigued me when I read about the way they punished members of their tribe who committed crimes. Real brutal stuff. But my favorite was the way they punished their women when they cheated. They tortured them terribly. You know what they did, Barn?"

"Made them listen to you ramble?"

Cordell ignored him. "They cut off their noses, Barn."

Denny started to say something smart and then realized what Cordell was saying. Thinking about it in that brief millisecond, Denny hoped Cordell wasn't talking about cutting off *his* nose.

"So that gave me an idea, Barn."

Here it came. Jesus.

"I've never cut off a nose before. I've cut off all kinds of stuff. I thought I had cut off everything a person could cut off a human. I mean, there were hands and feet and arms and dicks and tongues and ears. You name it. But you know what? No noses. Not one. Ever."

Denny felt his blood chill. Suddenly, he was terrified.

Cordell stared into his eyes and calmly said: "Until you."

Denny's eyes got big and his breath caught. He started to plead as he saw Cordell raising that blowgun again. He heard the *pfffft* sound, and he felt the dart pierce his chest. He looked down, seeing it there, and almost immediately things started to get blurry. He looked up at Cordell, managing only: "You fucker."

ELEVEN

DENNY'S EYES fluttered open and he saw light. The moment his eyes opened, he remembered his situation. His heart was already racing, and his mind immediately followed suit. He was lying on the table again in the torture room, strapped down. He tried to look down at his torso, but was unable to swivel his head far enough really to see anything. He turned his head far to the left where Cordell had been, but he wasn't there.

The room was empty except for Denny, who was unable to move. As usual, he could hear music playing from the radio in the next room. He knew the song, but couldn't immediately place it. Then it came to him – *Love Hurts*. Christ, he thought, immediately making the connection. What Cordell had done to him, and was about to do to him, all came as the result of Denny's love for Baby Allie.

Lying there in the empty room, Denny's thoughts turned to her. He could see her sweet, innocent face. He saw her fishing, trying to cast the line into the water, but doing so hesitantly as she was afraid of hooking herself or him. She had also been hesitant because she was leery of the worm on the hook. In fact, she had actually wept for the worm. In this moment, his mind was flooded with thoughts. Happy ones first – birthday parties, Mr Dinosaur, watching cartoons – and then sad, darker memories of her disappearance and of Cordell telling him he'd tortured and murdered her.

Denny's heart sank and he was once again overcome with grief. He wondered how it was possible that Allie's loss could still seem so fresh after all these years. And these newest revelations did nothing to ease his mind. Now he thought of Cordell's claims that he had eaten her. He thought of what Cordell had said about her waiting for a hero who would never come. And he thought of her dying alone, bleeding out from some horrible thing Cordell had done.

Denny was angry again. This was nothing new and would accomplish little as he was strapped here, completely in Cordell's control. And he thought of all the things he might do to Cordell were he to get free. A flurry of crazed, hyper-violent images came to him, but Denny knew the reality – if he ever did get free, there would be no fancy well-thought-out torture or execution. No, he would immediately snap and kill him with his bare hands. And that would be A-OK. He wouldn't need a ceremonious, flashy vengeance. Just the run-of-the-mill garden variety murder would do just fine. Thinking about this, Denny thought about the second reality – the *real* reality – that he would probably do nothing. Ever. Not only to Cordell, but in any capacity. The true likelihood was that Denny would only ever be tortured and die alone in this basement.

Dammit, he thought. This was not the way he wanted to die. He had always seen himself as a sort of badass hero figure, whether that perception was deserved or not. Denny knew that every man was the hero of his own story. Then he thought of Cordell, knowing full well Cordell saw himself as a hero, too.

The way Cordell saw it, he was a righteous man doing the bidding of God.

Stupid bastard.

Denny wasn't a particularly religious man. He wasn't an atheist either. The truth was that he didn't give a shit either way. But the thought of that idiot Cordell believing he was sent by God to punish him – to punish all those people; to punish Baby Allie – offended him to his very core. It wasn't anything about God that offended him, but the ridiculous delusion. It was Cordell's self-righteous justification of his own horribly wicked acts.

Thinking about this, Denny felt a longing in every fiber of his being that was stronger than any longing he'd ever known. He felt an overwhelming longing to hurt Cordell. To hurt him bad. Not torture, nothing fancy. Just punching his face in until it was just a bloody, dead pulp would suffice. But for now, all of this was a pipe dream. Denny could see no way he would be free anytime soon.

At that moment, Cordell walked in. Denny didn't hear him at first. He didn't know he was even there until he spoke. That little trick of startling him by speaking when Denny was unaware of his presence seemed to be Cordell's specialty. This simple thought angered Denny further. He knew none of these little things should have been enough to anger him so violently and tremendously, but certainly the combination of everything the motherfucker had done to him – had done to Allie – was enough to warrant it.

The thing Cordell said was, "Wakey-wakey, little buddy."

Denny turned his head to the left again, seeing the asshole standing there wearing a God's Gym muscle shirt. Not that Cordell had any muscles. No, his arms were fat and flabby. Even after having spent the past 13 years drinking himself into oblivion, Denny's arms were still more muscular and toned than Cordell's.

"Today is a big day, champ," said Cordell. "Today is the day I'm gonna do a magic show for you." He said this and then just stood there, staring at him, smiling a goofy smile. He obviously wanted Denny to ask what he was talking about, but Denny refused. Fuck him. There wasn't much Denny could, but refusing to answer was one thing, even if it was minor.

Cordell's smile started to fall away this time, and Denny could see that he was annoyed that he wouldn't play along.

"Big magic trick, Barn," he said. "You remember that game we all played when we were kids? The one where they pinched your nose and then held their thumb between their fingers to make it look like a nose? Remember that? They'd say: *I got your nose!*" Cordell laughed at this, the kind of laugh a person does when reminiscing. "You know what? One time, and this was when I was little, maybe five or so, mind you, my uncle did that to me. And you know what? I believed it, Barn! I know it's silly, but I really believed that fucker had taken my nose! It scared the bejeezus outta me and I cried like a baby. And he didn't say otherwise. He just laughed and laughed, repeating that: 'I got your nose, Cordell! I got your nose!'" Cordell looked at Denny, starting to grin again. "I never forgot that. Not ever. That's why I killed him. You know how I did it, Barn?"

Denny felt sick. He didn't want to hear any of this.

"I hit him in his face with an ax," said Cordell. "I shit you not." He paused, weighing his words, trying to make them sound dramatic, to give them a real storyteller's pizzazz. "You ever seen what an ax will do when you strike a man in the face with it?" His grin grew wider. "I suspect you haven't. Not many people have, truthfully. In that way, I'm kinda blessed. It ain't somethin' that comes up in everyday life. It's rare to see. But yeah, his whole fuckin' face just sort of crushed in and opened up." He giggled a giddy laugh. "That sucker *obliterated* his whole damn face!"

Denny lay there, his hand starting to throb again. He was sick of Cordell. "Just get it over with," he said.

Cordell just smiled, unfazed. "Hold your horses, Barney. We got time. Now, I'm sure you know where I'm going with that. That whole 'I got your nose' thing... I thought of that a few minutes ago and it made me chuckle, what with how I'm gonna cut your nose off. That's gonna be my magic trick. I'm gonna make your nose disappear!"

Denny felt an immense surge of fear, and his bladder loosened. He didn't urinate, but he could feel it shift, feel it loosen. "We don't have to do this," Denny pleaded.

"Oh, but we do," said Cordell, nodding. "We really do. That's why we're here. That's why God put us here together. You're the sinner and I'm the..." Cordell's face twisted and he looked away in thought. "Hmmm. I wonder what the correct term would be." He looked at Denny again. "What would you call me?"

"A fucking retard," said Denny. It was too easy. Low-hanging fruit. But Denny didn't care. There was nothing else he could do but call him names and try to piss him off, so he would do that until he could do it no more.

Cordell shook his head. "You never stop, do you? Anyway, where was I?" He thought for a second and then said, "Oh yeah, the nose. Here's an interesting bit of trivia: you ever hear that story about Michael Jackson? They say he didn't have a nose at the end of his life. I don't know if I believe it. I've never seen it confirmed. Like that Richard Gere gerbil thing, you know... But supposedly Mike had had so much plastic surgery, so many face-lifts, that he no longer had any nose cartilage. Something like that. I don't know. Noses aren't really my thing." He winked at Denny. "Not until today anyway."

"I hate you," spat Denny.

Cordell continued. "Supposedly Mike wore fake noses. I don't know where you get the noses though. I think about that sometimes. I mean, it's not like there's a nose department at K-Mart. You can't order noses off Amazon. But...supposedly he had these noses. Lots of 'em. I guess he could wear different noses on different days, maybe coordinate with his outfit. You know, how a person might change their shoes or their hat to match what they got on. Like women with purses. Well, that was him with noses. But here's the thing, and this applies to you, Barn. I guess when his nose was off, all he had was a gaping hole in the center of his face."

Denny felt sick, like he might vomit.

"You know how a skull has just got that hole there where the nose was?" asked Cordell. "Well, that's what Mike had." Cordell had been staring at Denny the whole time, but now his eyes seemed to zero in on his nose. He wasn't making a show of it, but it was obvious he was inspecting Denny's nose. "I think that's how you're gonna look, Barn. You'll just have that hole in the middle of your face. What do you think about that?"

Denny bucked hard against the straps, getting nowhere. He turned his head forward as he did. Then, finally, after he'd relaxed again, he reluctantly looked at Cordell.

"Please don't do this," he begged. *"I'm asking you as one human being to another. Please, Cordell."*

Cordell grinned again. "Got no choice, Barn. None at all. But I had a thought, and I think you're gonna enjoy this... You know how in the back of your mind you've still been thinking maybe you'll get free somehow and get outta here? Maybe even kill me?" He nodded, looking into Denny's eyes. "Yeah, I know you think that. Everyone thinks that. But no one ever does. But, here's the deal... Once I do this, once I cut off your nose, it won't matter. So what if you get loose? What are you gonna do out there, Barn? Your life will pretty much be over. No one will ever be able to look at your face again without feeling the urge to vomit."

"*Why?*" asked Denny. "Really, *why?* Do we really need to do this?"

Cordell nodded solemnly. "There's no choice. None at all. It's outta my hands. But I want you to know something. It's not personal. Not personal at all."

Denny glared at him. "It feels pretty personal to me."

Cordell nodded, the grin still on his face. "I imagine it does."

The two of them looked at one another for a moment. Then, unexpectedly, Cordell raised his hand so Denny could see it. He was holding a small handsaw.

In that moment, Denny was seized by fear. His eyes got big, his pulse sped up, he could hardly breathe. He felt like pissing himself. It was all bad. All of it.

"*Please, Cordell,*" he said.

Cordell leaned in over him, raising the saw before his face. "Time to make the doughnuts," he said. Leaning in, Cordell put the saw teeth against the bridge of Denny's nose. There were tears in Denny's eyes. "*Please!*"

"I would say this won't hurt a bit, but that would be a lie," said Cordell.

"*Please, no. Please.*"

And Cordell started to saw. The teeth began to rip into Denny's flesh. The pain was searing and incredible, somehow a million times worse than the pain he'd felt when Cordell had cut off his finger. Denny screamed in agony as the teeth of the saw ground their way through cartilage. Denny screamed loudly, but Cordell just kept sawing, slowly, deliberately. Denny saw the blood spurt forward, flying onto Cordell's grinning, determined face.

As Denny bucked with pain, Cordell applied more pressure, pinning his head down against the table. The blade had half the nose off now. Denny kept screaming in agony. Not words, just a high-pitched, shrill scream. Even as he screamed, he could hear the saw making its way through his nose.

Cordell was saying something about sadism. About the origin of the word. But Denny didn't care. He couldn't focus on that. He just kept bucking and screaming, and Cordell kept rambling, laughing, and sawing.

Finally, thankfully, Denny slipped into unconsciousness.

TWELVE

Denny was still strapped down when he was awakened by the blowtorch cauterizing the wound where his nose had been. He couldn't be entirely sure, but it seemed like he had been screaming even before he woke up. He was certainly screaming now. He didn't know how long any of this torturous shit had lasted. It was probably only a few minutes, but it felt like a goddamn eternity. It was a horror show. All of it, from the searing heat to the immense pain from his gaping facial wound to the shitty Captain & Tennille song playing in the next room. It was surreal, like a fever dream. A really, really terrible, really intense fever dream. Denny could feel his sanity slipping away during this continuous stretch of pain. He made a conscious decision to scream out again but realized he was already screaming. And crying. Crying hard. It was terrible. He thought maybe he should pray to God for help, but he couldn't compose himself enough to do so. So he just screamed and screamed as he could do nothing else.

Finally, after the longest, most agonizing period of pain he'd ever endured , he passed out again.

When he woke up some time later, he was back in his room, lying chained and naked on the floor. His face hurt. In fact, his whole head hurt. All of it. Just all of it. He was moaning from the moment his eyes popped open. He didn't have the strength to move much, so he just lay there weeping. Now he had the composure to say a prayer in his head, so he prayed for death. But death did not come. At least, he thought, it would come soon. It had to. As he lay there weeping and hurting, he felt his stomach buckle. The hot, acidic vomit rose up in his throat. Lying there, he worried he might choke, but he didn't have the strength to sit up. He turned his head just in time, and several gulps of vomit heaved from his lips on to the floor. He curled up into the fetal position, his chains rattling as he did, and closed his eyes, hurting and longing for a death that would not come.

The pain was intense and he could barely focus on anything else. He saw Baby Allie in his mind, just as she had been at seven, but there were no clear coherent thoughts. Just images. Then his mind turned to the other dead members of his family. Again, there were no clear thoughts. Just images. He felt pangs of guilt and sadness, which combined with the various pains and the sickness in his stomach. He lay there weeping. As he did, one logical thought occurred to him: What would he lose next? What appendage would Cordell cut off his body tomorrow? And then a second thought followed: Would it be tomorrow? Or was today already tomorrow? He had no way of knowing how long he'd been unconscious, but thought it likely that the severity of trauma to his body would have made him sleep longer. Frightened and tired, Denny curled his body up even tighter.

He wanted to die so very badly. He did. He didn't even care. This led him to wonder about God and whether or not he existed. At this moment Denny considered it likely that he did not. He certainly hadn't seen his hand in his own life. At least not in any positive way. God hadn't reached down from the heavens and saved his family. He hadn't come down and saved Baby Allie. Nor had he sent his angels to this basement to save Denny. But hell, Denny thought, he himself was the least of the victims. If God hadn't saved them, why would he waste his time on a fuck-up like him? And in that moment it occurred to Denny that if there was indeed a God, he hated him now. Why should he love a deity that had inflicted so much pain and suffering on him and everyone he'd ever loved? But then he considered that, according to the Bible, Jesus himself had endured tremendous sufferings, even being crucified. But this didn't change Denny's mindset. If anything, it made him believe that Jesus was weak. Who, if given the chance to do otherwise, would willingly lay down his life for a deity who didn't care about him? Or, even worse, an ideal? A concept. It was all bullshit. Maybe his view was distorted by the pain and trauma, but in this moment Denny concluded there was no God. And if there was a God, well, he could fuck right off.

Denny lay there for hours, awake and hurting, moaning and crying. He was no longer concerned with getting loose or inflicting pain on Cordell. All he wanted was to stop hurting. To stop existing. Lying there, not trying to focus on it, not focusing on anything really, he considered the possibility that Cordell might eat him once he was dead. *Good,* he thought. *I hope the fucker chokes.*

Finally, after what seemed like days but may have only been hours, Denny heard the upstairs door open. This was followed by the sounds of Cordell's footfalls on the stairs. Throughout this, Denny remained lying on the floor, curled up in a ball, hurting. He heard Cordell at the bottom of the stairs, approaching now, and he heard the rustling of the dog food bag.

"I'm really sorry, Barn," he heard Cordell say, but he didn't turn to look at him. "I had no choice. Not that I minded it, mind you. But it wasn't my choice. Really it wasn't." Then Denny heard the sound of the dog food pieces sliding across the floor towards him.

The Moody Blues were singing *Nights in White Satin*. It occurred to Denny, randomly, that this song was a few years older than the others the station normally played. It was a strange thought to have at this moment, but it was a thought he had nonetheless.

"It's gonna be okay, Barn," said Cordell. "There's an upside to all this, you know."

Silence. Cordell obviously waiting for a response.

"You wanna know what that is?"

More silence.

Cordell laughed a sickening laugh. "The upside is that you can't see your face. It really is hideous. Ridiculously hideous. I mean, you go out in public, you go to the mall, you're gonna make little kids cry. They're gonna go home and have night-mares about your face." Cordell chuckled again. "Your face is beyond grotesque. Worse than the fucking Elephant Man. Far worse. Like, if the Elephant Man's head caught on fire and both his eyes popped out. Really disgusting shit, Barn. Vomit-inducing."

Denny lay there, turned away, crying in silence. He would not give the fucker the satisfaction of seeing him cry. He would not speak.

"Guess you're not talkin' to me, huh?" said Cordell. "Shame. Can't say as I blame you though. If someone cut off my nose and made me look like a freak show attraction, I'd prob-ably be pissed, too." He laughed again, obviously enjoying the sound of his own laughter.

Denny hated the sonofabitch more than he had hated him before. As Cordell continued yapping, it occurred to Denny that he should have prayed that God kill Cordell rather than save or kill himself. And then he remembered his having decided that there was no God.

"I wish you could see your face, Barn," said Cordell. "You know when people say, 'If you could see the look on your face'? Well, it's true. And I don't think you'd like it if you could. No, no, not at all. Not one bit." Cordell laughed again, this time more of a giggle. "Makes me think of another saying. You probably know this one. You ever hear someone talk about someone cutting off their nose to spite their face? Well, you spited the shit outta your face!"

Denny lay there, hating him, wishing he would go away. He wanted to fight, wanted to scream, but refused. He wouldn't do it. He absolutely would not. If he could do nothing else, he could refuse to play along. Fuck Cordell. Fuck him and his bullshit God who told him to cut off Denny's nose and murder Baby Allie. Fuck everyone. Denny no longer cared about anyone or anything. Nothing mattered anymore. Not God, not himself, not anything.

He hadn't heard Cordell's feet on the stairs yet, so he assumed he was still standing there grinning, trying to come up with more clever shit to say. Denny could feel his anger swelling by the second, threatening to override his decision to remain silent. *He'd better leave or else*, thought Denny. But what? He could do nothing and he knew it. This realization made him even angrier.

"Doesn't matter anyway," said Cordell. "Tomorrow's gonna be another big day for you, pal. You wanna act like a jerk? Fine. Then you'll get treated like one. You think today was bad, you ain't seen nothin' yet. Tomorrow's gonna be way, way worse. Tomorrow's gonna be one for the record books. I'm gonna hurt you in ways you can't even imagine. I'm gonna get real creative, Barn. I don't even know what I'm gonna do yet. I'm gonna stay up tonight and think about it. Maybe look around on the internet and see if I can find some more creative ways to dismember you." He paused and then said, sounding light like he was trying to be funny: "Goodnight, Barn. Nighty-night, old buddy."

Denny lay there, listening to Cordell make his way back up the stairs. When he reached the top, Denny heard the door close.

Denny hated Cordell. He wanted very badly to do something to get at him, but he could think of nothing he could do. Before, he had been ready to die, but now his mindset had reverted to wanting to hurt Cordell or at the very least anger him. While Cordell was sitting upstairs trying to devise some new way to torture him, Denny would be down here in the basement trying to come up with a way to strike back.

There had to be something, he thought. *There had to be.*

THIRTEEN

He lay there in pain, squeezing his eyes closed, trying to lose himself in the darkness, as if not looking at this awful basement might somehow make it less real. Maybe if he kept his eyes closed, he could imagine he was somewhere else. Somewhere where he was free. A place where he still had his dignity. A place where he still had all his fingers and his face wasn't disfigured. Maybe Baby Allie would be there, too.

Yes, he could see it now. He saw him and Allie, playing in the park. She was still seven and he still believed he was a decent man. Sure, he was lying to himself, but it was a much easier lie to swallow back then. The sun was out and Denny was slogging through the day, slowed by the humidity. But not Allie. No, like the seven-year-old she was, she continued full steam ahead. Denny thought he'd probably had that familiar thought where he'd wished he had as much energy as she did, but he didn't know for sure. Couldn't remember specifics. But there were other things he could remember. He remembered pushing her on the swing, Allie screaming: *"Higher, Denny-Pa, higher!"* He remembered her begging him to go down the slide with her and him trying to explain that slipper slides were much harder for grownups than they were for kids. In his mind's eye, Denny saw the girl riding on his back as he pretended to be a dinosaur. *"Go, Mr Dinosaur, Go!"* she happily cried. Denny had been happy, too. It seemed like a foreign concept now, but it was true. It had been an easier time. It was a time he enjoyed looking back on. Unlike now. If he survived this, which he didn't believe he would, there would be never be a time when he would look back on this fondly. Not ever.

I'd Really Love to See You Tonight was playing now, and Denny thought about how the song related to Baby Allie. Thinking of her, remembering that day in the park, he really did want to see her. More than anything.

Thinking about Allie and the park and Mr Dinosaur, Denny wondered if this was an authentic memory. Had all that really been one single trip to the park, or had it merely been a "best of" collage of memories from various visits? It no longer mattered. The distinction was pointless. No one else could have possibly known the answer to that question but Denny and Allie, and Allie was dead. Now those once-happy memories only served to torture him.

This thought made him grimace. "Torture him." Denny had always been the kind of man who clung to memories that injured him emotionally, but none of that was real torture. He'd always believed it was, but he'd been wrong. Now Denny knew all too well what real torture was. That other stuff had been folly. But this was something different. Something darker. Something macabre. These past few days with Cordell had been something he could never have imagined. Not that he would have wanted to.

Lying there with his eyes clamped shut, Denny weighed his options. He considered ways that he might escape, none of which seemed realistic. He was helpless here. There was seemingly nothing he could do. Even if he could just make things the slightest bit difficult for Cordell, Denny would see that as a victory. A minor victory, but a victory nonetheless.

Denny wanted to hurt the bastard. Wanted to claw his eyes out. Wanted to curb stomp the motherfucker, splitting his skull in half. He could imagine no death too gruesome or too severe for this asshole. No, Cordell had to die. He *needed* to die. Sure, he would die someday like everyone else, maybe from natural causes, but that seemed unfair. That wasn't enough by a country mile. This sonofabitch had to die badly. He had to die one of those deaths the bad guys died at the end of a nineties action movie. Cordell deserved it all. He deserved to be decapitated. He deserved to have his eyeballs popped from his head as his skull was crushed. He deserved...

Denny stopped himself. What good were these fantasies? They were pointless and counterproductive. If Denny was to make any mark at all, he needed to focus and find a way – or better yet, *ways* – to hurt Cordell. At the very least inconvenience him.

Fuck Cordell. Fuck him hard, in every goddamn orifice. The thought of his stupid face and his terrible, grotesque grin made Denny want to rip his face from his skull. *Dammit...*

Denny started to open his eyes, but was startled by the brightness of the overhead light and clamped them shut again. No, he thought. Darkness was better. And in that moment, he realized there was one tiny thing he could do to at least anger Cordell. A tiny thing, but a thing nonetheless. Denny opened his eyes. Lying on his back, he was staring up at the overhead light. Could he reach the light if he jumped for it? Sure, he thought. But the chains would make it difficult. They would weigh him down like an anchor. Thinking of this, he considered the possibility that trying to make the jump – successful or no – could hurt him further. Denny wasn't sure he could handle that. After all, he wasn't in the best shape. It wasn't just the years of abuse he'd done to his body, but more the days of abuse Cordell had done.

Still...

Thinking about it further, Denny thought he could jump up there and strike that light, breaking the bulb. There would be downsides. Downsides for sure. He would then be enveloped in darkness and there would be glass all over the floor. Glass that would cut not only his feet but also every other part of his naked body that touched it. But then, he thought, what was a little glass? Surely a glass cut to his feet or his legs or his back or even his balls would pale in comparison to having had his nose sawed off. Thinking of this, Denny concluded that he had endured about as much as a man could endure. At this point, all this other shit would be a cake walk. This was nothing.

And again, fuck Cordell.

So yes, he decided, he would jump and try to break that light. For the briefest of moments, he thought it might empower him. And it would, but so marginally it might not be worth it. But he would not go down without fighting. Not ever. And if he couldn't hurt Cordell, then the least he could do was break that goddamn light.

He stared up at it. In his mind, he could see himself breaking it. But he could also see the shards of glass on the floor when he inevitably tried to sit or lie down. But it would be worth it, wouldn't it? Again, it was a tiny thing, but sometimes the tiny things mattered most. If there was any way he could get at Cordell at all, he had to do it, didn't he? He felt he owed it to Cordell to be disobedient. To be defiant. To stand strong in the face of whatever bullshit he might throw his way.

So, for now, there was the light. It's all there was, but in this moment, it was enough. Denny stood, swaying as he did. His body ached. His face and his hand still hurt tremendously, but the pain had subsided a little. Well, not subsided, he thought, so much as become dull from being so constant. Denny looked up at the light again. It wasn't that far over his head. So yes, he would break that fucking light. He would shatter it to pieces. Perhaps it accomplished nothing practical, but it would at least give him the tiny satisfaction of knowing he'd done the only thing he'd been capable of doing.

He stared up at that light. As he did, he raised his shackled arms up high. He braced himself. He bent his knees a bit, on the balls of his feet now, ready to spring. He tensed his muscles in preparation. And he jumped, swatting at the light. He missed the fucker and wound up swinging just beneath it. Worse, he stumbled when he landed, injuring his ankle.

Dammit, he thought. He wouldn't give up. Aside from his ankle, the jump hadn't affected his body as much as he'd anticipated. He raised his arms again, setting himself, still staring at the light. He bent his knees a bit, on the balls of his feet again, and he leaped, making contact this time. The bulb shattered and the light itself swung away from him. Pieces of glass fell to the floor in the darkness and for the briefest of moments Denny felt as if he'd accomplished something. He felt like he'd won.

But now, standing in the darkness, afraid to move for fear of cutting himself, he didn't feel like he was as much a victor as he had before. After standing in the darkness for a moment, he finally eased himself down to the ground, sitting with his legs crossed, his drooping testicles touching the floor. Somehow he'd gotten lucky and had managed to do this without cutting himself. Despite this fact, he wasn't ready to stretch out or lie down just yet. He knew the glass was still there and that getting cocky would lead to him getting cut. He didn't figure Cordell would sweep up the glass, instead leaving it there to make Denny pay for his insolence. So he would not be able to avoid it. Denny would be cut eventually. Probably many times. That was the reality and he was fine with it, but he was in no hurry for it to occur. So, in the meantime he would sit and wait in the darkness.

He was still sitting with his legs crossed, hours later, when the door opened. Light poured in from the upstairs world, and Cordell's silhouette stood in the door frame. *"You stupid fucker!"* he yelled. "Did you do this? Did you break the light, or did it just burn out?" Cordell waited, somehow still believing he was gonna receive a response.

Finally, he said: "You dumb piece of shit," and he disappeared briefly, the door still open. A moment later he reappeared with a lit flashlight. He started down the stairs in the darkness.

"You shouldn't have done this, Barney," he said, sounding menacing. "You really shouldn't have. You don't know what you've done." Denny heard Cordell chuckle, moving closer, making his way down the stairs. "Believe it or not, I was being nice before. But not now. Not if you broke the light. I'm sure you think you've accomplished something here, but you have no power, Barn. None." His voice was becoming angrier as he continued. "You are not in charge here. *I am in charge! Do you hear me?! I'm the goddamn boss! Do you hear me, Barn?! Do you fucking hear me?!*"

Denny sat in the darkness, saying nothing. The moving flashlight was almost to the bottom of the stairs. This made Denny nervous. He stood, preparing himself for whatever Cordell might do. The light moved closer, shining on the floor. Then, when Cordell was only a couple feet away from him, the flashlight beam came up, shining into Denny's eyes.

"You did this, didn't you?" asked Cordell. "I shoulda

known. I knew there was something different about you. Something asshole-ish. Something jerky."

Denny backed up, trying to see if Cordell would come too close, no longer seeing the boundaries of the chains. This could go both ways. Not being able to see Cordell, Denny had no way of knowing what weapons Cordell might possibly be holding in his other hand. But fuck it. No pain, no gain. Cordell came closer – close enough that Denny was sure he could reach him – and shined the light down on the glass.

"You dumb bastard," said Cordell. He started to say something else, but Denny lunged towards him, grabbing his head with his hands. He was really doing this. This was happening. Cordell's head was really in his hands. Cordell let out a screech and the flashlight dropped, rolling away. Denny had Cordell. The fucker was fighting, but Denny wasn't gonna let him get away. He tightened his grip on his head, pulling him closer. When he had Cordell's head against his chest, he wrapped the chains from his wrists around his neck, pulling them tight. Cordell wasn't saying anything smart now. He just gurgled and groaned. Doubling down, Denny swiveled back, hefting the choking Cordell up and back with him. Cordell struggled, trying to fight, but Denny could feel the fight leaving him. When he sensed Cordell was close to death, he found his second wind and leaned back further, choking him harder.

And just like that, Cordell was dead. Shocked and unsure what had just happened and what would occur now, Denny stood there for a long moment with the dead man limp in his arms.

FOURTEEN

Standing there in the darkness, Denny knew he was fucked. This situation was beyond bad. He'd believed he was saving himself, but realized now he had only made things worse. For starters, the flashlight had rolled away, out of his reach. Now its beam shone directly on to a wall on the opposite side of the room, doing him no good. With Cordell gone, there would be no light or food. No chance of escape. Things had gone from bad to worse, the classic "out of the frying pan into the fire" scenario.

He'd scarfed down his food immediately after Cordell had brought it the previous day. Was it the previous day? Or was it today? Denny didn't know. He did, however, know he was hungry. But then he'd been hungry since he'd first arrived. A cupful of dog food a day, as it turned out, was not enough to feed an adult man adequately. Luckily, there was still water in the large bowl – also made for dogs – that Cordell had provided. But that wouldn't last. And Denny would have to be careful maneuvering in the darkness, or he could spill the water. Then even that would be gone.

He dropped Cordell's body, letting it fall to his feet. Fleetwood Mac's *The Chain* was playing now. At any other moment, he would have enjoyed the song. But for now it only added to the chaos. Further, the music served as a cruel reminder that there was a real world out there somewhere. A world where normal people ate real meals, went to work each day, fell in and out of love, and did all this without being chained to a wall. Also, there was daylight. It had only been two or three days since Denny had been outside, but he missed fresh air. He missed sunlight. And most of all, he missed freedom.

Standing there, feeling Cordell's body against his foot, a thought occurred to him. Maybe the keys to the shackles were in Cordell's pocket. That, he thought, would be terrific. The best thing ever. Before this thought had fully registered, his shackled hands were already moving, his knees bending, bringing him down closer to the body. Grabbing, he felt Cordell's shirt. His hands made their way along the body, searching for pockets. After a moment of fumbling, he discovered one. He twisted his hand, snaking it in, but found nothing but a few loose pieces of candy. They felt like either M&Ms or Skittles, but he couldn't be sure. His heart sank at not finding keys, but he also felt a modicum of excitement at having discovered the candy. He popped the pieces into his mouth. M&Ms. He would have preferred Skittles, but was happy just to taste something that wasn't blood or dog food.

He moved his hands around the torso, locating the second pocket. He pushed his fingers in, finding a wallet. This wasn't helpful. His fingers kept moving, and he found something else. Something sharp and metallic he immediately identified as keys. He would be free! His heart sped up and his mind raced as he retrieved the key ring, which felt as if it had four, maybe five keys on it. He fumbled with them in his right hand, bringing them up to the cuff on his left wrist. He isolated the first key, searched for the lock on the cuff, and tried to insert it. The key didn't fit. *Shit.* He then moved on to the second key. Same deal. Then the third. The fourth. The fifth. None fit. He started to panic, started to breathe harder, but thought maybe in the darkness he'd missed a key, maybe even tried the same one twice. So he tried them all again, but still none worked. Then he switched wrists, going through the motions again with that lock, but none of the keys worked there either.

Feeling frustrated and doomed, Denny looked up at the ceiling and screamed out, *"No!"* repeatedly. He roared it four times. When he stopped, the silence was deafening. He considered screaming again, but cried instead. Angry, he hurled the keys at a wall in the darkness, hearing them strike with a clanging sound and then fall to the floor. Overcome with despair and feeling disoriented, he shuffled in place, trying to sidestep the body. As he did, he felt a sharp piece of glass pierce the soft skin on the bottom of his right foot. Startled by the unexpected pain, Denny yelped and stumbled back. As he did, it occurred to him that he would probably step on another piece of glass if he continued to move.

He looked up towards the ceiling, unable to see it. Elton John was playing. Something about *Daniel.* Staring up, searching for a God, Denny wept, falling to his knees. "Please," he begged. "Please..." He didn't finish the request, knowing if there was a God and if he could hear him, he would understand. Now on his knees, Denny leaned forward, falling over Cordell's body, weeping. He clutched the dead man instinctively, like a child to his mother. He hated Cordell, and Cordell was dead, but it felt good to touch another human. He continued to weep, harder and harder, heaving as he did. Eventually he realized he was wailing, which caused him to cry harder.

Denny had felt despair in these past few days, had felt

despair over the past 13 years, but this was beyond all that. This transcended despair. Now there was the certain fact he would die alone in the dark, surrounded by death and shit.

A number of hours passed with Denny crying, praying, pissing, shitting, sleeping – he thought he'd slept, but wasn't entirely sure – and everything was the same save for the songs on the radio. A happy DJ, comfortably sitting somewhere in a nice, shackle-free studio, occasionally came on to crack jokes or give his limited insights on world events. Earlier in the day, he had shared an anecdote about the members of Deep Purple meeting the Queen of England. That had been a high point in a day of infinite pain and sorrow. Denny didn't give a shit about either Deep Purple or the Queen of fucking England, but it had been nice to escape his confines for the briefest of moments, imagining those people doing those things. He didn't pay that much attention to the radio anymore, but he did hear some things. After all, it was hard not to hear them when there were no other stimuli in this dark hell. And when he listened, literally everything he heard was a reminder of things he would never do again. Because literally everything the songs or the deejay discussed were things outside this basement hell. There were no songs about shackles and shit and dead bodies. At least not on this station.

Eventually he could shed no more tears. His tear ducts had dried. His face still hurt terribly and Denny was sure his sleep had only been his passing out from the pain. His finger was starting to hurt less. It hurt like a bitch, but its pain was tremendously less than that of his nose. And now his knuckles were bloody and hurting as Denny had punched the floor repeatedly. This had accomplished nothing, but who cared? Nothing he would do would accomplish anything ever again. His life was over.

Sitting there, he wondered if there was a heaven or hell. He highly doubted it and didn't care either way. He was ready to just die and get it over with. But if those things did exist, would he go to heaven? Denny considered this but didn't really care either way. He remembered all the talk of fire and brimstone and the gnashing of teeth, but he could see no way hell could be worse than this.

He slept again. He was sure of it. But how long had it been? There was no way to know. And the deejay on the radio never seemed to mention days or times, so Denny was lost in a perpetual cycle of darkness, pain, stench, and seventies soft rock.

Billy Joel was singing now. Denny liked Billy Joel. He'd always considered him an intelligent songwriter. Maybe it was because he sang about fancy parties and living in New York City. He had a song about an Italian restaurant. Things that had seemed foreign and exotic to Denny, who'd just lived in Kansas City, subsisting on cheeseburgers and pizza.

But now Billy Joel, singing that goofy doo-wop song, sounded distant and surreal. Today (tonight?) he did not enjoy listening to him. None of the music the radio played provided him the slightest bit of joy or satisfaction.

When Denny got bored, which was pretty much all the time, he would stare at the flashlight lying in the distance, shining its beam on nothing. Occasionally he would feel frightened that something – maybe some sort of boogeyman – would emerge from the shadows. But what boogeyman could be worse than the one he'd slain? And if a monster or boogeyman did kill him, it would be a welcome reprieve.

Denny masturbated a couple of times. He didn't feel good about it, sitting down here naked among piles of shit beside a dead body, but he'd done it. There had been nothing else to do and his penis had become irrationally erect. When he masturbated, he could think of nothing particularly pleasing to focus on, so he'd done it on autopilot, doing it simply to do it. The third time he attempted this, the act was interrupted by the thought of what he looked like doing it; naked and flabby and dirty and bloody and missing a nose. The thought disgusted him and he lost his erection. He then vowed to stop masturbating.

Eventually his hunger began to override everything else and he started to consider eating Cordell. He didn't want to and the thought sickened him, but his body had an irrational motivation to survive. His mind recognized this was stupid. After all, even if he did this disgusting, horrific thing, he would still die. But his raging hunger forced the issue. He would hold out, he thought. He would not eat Cordell.

Not long after, the realization of what he'd done when he'd thrown the keys dawned on him. He could have used their sharp edges to slice his wrists. He could have killed himself. He could have left this place. *Fuck, fuck, fuck.* With this thought, his sadness multiplied tenfold. The thought sickened him so much that it eventually caused him to vomit again. He didn't want to eat Cordell, but his body somehow knew enough to vomit away from the body.

The water ran out first. That was when Denny absolutely knew that things had become dire. What would he do now?

He thought of Cordell again. If he ate his body, maybe the moisture and blood would replenish him. Could that work? Was that possible? Denny didn't know, didn't really think so, but could see no other option.

Eventually his hunger and thirst became so great that he knew there was no other way. Where the thought of eating Cordell had previously repulsed him, he no longer cared.

So Denny started to eat Cordell's now-rotting body. He had no way to cut the meat loose, so he had to lean down over the body and tear the meat with his teeth, like an animal.

He started with Cordell's arm. The meaty, flabby part. He knew he should be sickened by the taste, but his taste buds were so longing for flavor that Cordell tasted amazing. Even better, he satiated his hunger. But this did nothing to satisfy Denny's tremendous thirst. He was also starting to feel weak, and he knew it was the lack of water.

Denny did this for a while. Hours, maybe days. He didn't know. Alternating between eating Cordell's flesh – his throat, his face, his arms and legs – and sleeping and defecating. But he did not masturbate, just as he'd vowed. Besides, he could no longer afford to lose precious bodily fluids.

He was incredibly weak.

He was sleeping, actually dreaming, which he never did – a dream about playing catch with his dead son Timmy – when the upstairs door awakened him.

FIFTEEN

The sound was startling. He sat upright, looking up the stairs. The door was open, its light pouring in, and it looked like a solitary square of light floating in a sea of darkness. The light was bright, blinding him. He blinked, trying to accustom his eyes to the glare. Denny hadn't seen light of any kind since the flashlight beam had gone out what he believed were days ago. He guessed it had been days, but couldn't say for sure.

He could see a silhouetted figure standing in the center of the light.

"Daddy?" asked the voice. It was a woman. Denny concluded it must have been Cordell's daughter. His first inclination had been to answer, momentarily thinking it was Evelyn. But as quickly as that thought occurred, it disappeared as Denny remembered she was dead.

Staring up at her, he wondered if this woman would be a friend or foe. Probably foe considering he'd killed and eaten the majority of her father. But maybe she didn't know what went on down here. Maybe she was unaware that her father had been keeping captives in the basement and torturing them to death.

"Daddy?" came the voice again.

Denny sat in silence, wondering what to do. Finally, he mustered up the courage to say: "Can you help me?"

The figure stood in silence for a moment, trying to understand. "Who...*who are you?"*

"I'm hurt bad," he croaked, his voice dry. "I need help. Please...*help me."*

Hearing his words, Denny realized he sounded more desperate than he wanted to. But it couldn't be helped. The reality was that he *was* desperate. So desperate that he'd been subsisting on the rotten remains of a dead man. He was naked and badly injured. He had no pinky finger and, even worse, no nose.

"Who are you?" she asked, sounding uneasy.

"My name is Denny Davis," he managed. "Please. Please help me. Please. I'm hurt bad. He... He cut off my nose."

"Where is he?" she asked. It immediately registered with Denny that she knew exactly who he meant when he'd said that, and also that she didn't sound at all surprised. These were not good signs.

"He's down here," said Denny.

"Is he... Is he *okay?"*

"He's dead."

The woman stood there for a long moment. Being only a silhouetted figure, Denny couldn't see her reaction. But he sensed apprehension.

"Call the police," he said. "Please. They'll take care of this."

The silhouetted figure moved, slowly at first, kind of shuffling around, and then turned and left. The door was still standing open, and for a moment there was only the light. Then the woman returned.

"What's wrong with the light down there?" she asked.

"It's..." Denny started to speak, but his voice was so dry that he choked. A moment later he finished. "It's out."

"Oh," she said. Then she started down the stairs. Denny could hear the steps creaking, one by one. She slowly made her way down the steps towards him. He wondered why she was doing this instead of calling the cops. If she called them, this whole nightmare could be behind them in a few minutes. They would come and take care of all this. Denny would never have a nose again, but maybe he could get one of those prosthetic noses Cordell had mentioned.

When the woman was about halfway down, a flashlight beam came alive, shining towards the bottom of the stairs. *She was holding a flashlight!* The beam bounced around as she made her way down. When she was near the bottom, the beam shone into Denny's face, blinding him. He was still sitting on the ground with Cordell's body beside him.

"You look terrible," said the woman.

"I need help. He hurt me really bad."

"Hmmm." That was all she said, and Denny didn't know how to interpret this. She was at the bottom of the steps now. Denny couldn't see her, but he could place her voice and see where the flashlight beam was. The beam made its way down to Cordell's remains. Denny looked at it and was repulsed by what he saw. He knew what he'd been doing, but the darkness had obscured just how grotesque it was.

"Fuck," said the woman, and then he heard her gag. As she did, the beam dropped a bit, bouncing as she heaved. A moment passed, the woman apparently regaining her composure, and then the light came back up to Denny, bright in his eyes.

"Please," he said.

"What did you do?" asked the voice, sounding angry.

"I had to," he said, pleading. "He didn't give me any choice. He chained me up. He cut off my finger." Denny raised his shackled hand to show her the stump. "See? And he cut off my nose. *The fucker cut off my nose!*"

The beam of light stayed in his face and there was a long silence. Denny had no idea what the woman might be thinking. He stood to face her.

"I'm surprised you're still alive," she said, calm and matter-of-factly. "Daddy don't usually let folks live."

Denny looked at her, where he knew her face must be, just above the light. *"You knew?"*

"Knew what?"

Denny stood there, staring. "What he was doing down here," he said.

She laughed, and Denny became afraid. What was this? What would happen now?

"Of course I knew," she said. "Daddy was doing God's work. Daddy was teaching the sinners. He was helping them repent."

Denny cocked his head, squinting towards her. *"Helping them repent by murdering them?"*

The light came closer. The woman was close, and Denny wondered what was happening. When the taser touched his chest, he didn't know what it was. He jumped at first, but not as much as he did a few seconds later when she electrocuted him.

SIXTEEN

DENNY'S EYES fluttered open and he knew immediately where he was. He was strapped down to the table where Cordell had removed his finger and nose. This was like a terrible version of *Groundhog's Day*, where Denny was being forced to relive the same godawful day, day in, day out. As his eyes adjusted to the light, he felt his heart sink. Any chance of a reprieve now seemed lost.

"Good, you're awake," said the woman, now beside him. He turned his head towards her, seeing a plastic glass of water with a straw extended towards him. His eyes went immediately to the straw as it moved towards his lips. When it touched his mouth, he felt so overwhelmed with joy that he might have wept had he had the bodily fluids to do so. He gulped the water down. It was incredible.

"Not so fast," said the woman. "If you drink too fast, you'll make yourself even sicker. That's what happened to the prisoners from the concentration camps. Do you know that story?" Denny removed his mouth from the straw. He didn't want to stop drinking, but he knew she was right. He looked at her as she said, "The German soldiers had already gone, leaving the Jews behind. When the American GI's came to liberate them, they gave them food and water and the Jews ate and drank too quickly, and that made them ill. A lot of them died."

As she spoke, Denny stared at her face. And he knew. The red hair was a dead giveaway, but not as much as her face. Staring at her, he recognized the features as being an older version of those he saw each day in his memories. He gasped, staring.

It was Baby Allie! She was older now, but it was her, alive and well!

His heart soared and he could hardly breathe.

She saw the look in his eyes.

"*What?*" she asked. "Why are you staring at me like that?"

His voice was trembling as he said, "I know you. I...*know* you."

She stared back, confused.

"I don't know what you're talking about," she said.

Again, he would have wept if he could.

"Don't you remember me?" he asked.

Her expression turned into something stern, bordering on anger. "I recognize you as the motherfucker who killed my daddy. The man who *ate* my daddy."

Daddy! She believed Cordell was her father! Hearing this, Denny was overcome with many emotions, all at once.

"No, Allie," he said. "Cordell was *not* your father."

She glared at him. "My name isn't Allie."

He stared at her, feeling his bottom lip quivering. He didn't speak because he didn't know what to say.

"My name is Ruth. I was named after Ruth, from the Bible. She was a Moab who married an Israelite. She eventually saved Naomi, her mother, and won the love of Boaz. She was an ancestor of Christ."

"*No,*" Denny blurted. "Your name is Allie Davis. Your mother's name was Evelyn Davis. You were born in Kansas City, Missouri."

She glared at him. "That's bullshit," she said. "*Why are you saying this?*"

"Because it's true, Allie. Every word."

"No," she said defiantly. "Cordell was my daddy. This is where I've always lived."

Denny lay there, his head twisted to the left so he could see her. He contemplated her statement and then asked, "Who's your mother?"

She smiled, smiling big, but Denny didn't know why.

Then she said, "I don't have a mother. I came directly from God. I was his gift to my daddy for all his hard work."

"*No!*" Denny blurted. "You were kidnapped when you were seven. That piece of shit Cordell kidnapped you from a McDonald's in Rolla, Missouri. You and me, we were on a camping trip. Don't you remember?"

She stood there, staring, saying nothing. Denny could see the wheels of her mind turning. She was thinking about it.

"You *do* remember," Denny said. "I can see it on your face."

She glared, doubling down. "I remember *nothing*. I'm the daughter of Cordell Dennings. I am a literal gift from God. I'm...*special.*"

"Yes," said Denny, trying to nod but finding difficulty at this angle and in his straps. "You *are* special. But you're special for other reasons. You're my granddaughter. My Baby Allie. You're the daughter of Evelyn, my daughter."

There were tears in Allie's eyes now and Denny could see she was trembling.

"You remember," he said. "I can see it. *You remember.*"

"Stop!"

"Cordell kidnapped you. He stole you."

"I said stop!" she screamed. *"Stop now!"*

"You ordered Chicken McNuggets. You were coloring a picture of a Dalmatian dressed like a fireman."

Her expression changed and Denny could clearly see recognition, as if the Dalmation coloring page had somehow done the trick.

"I can see it on your face!" he said. *"I can see it! You remember, Allie! You remember!"*

"No!" she screamed.

He started to speak again, to tell her about her mother, but Allie snapped, *"Just shut up! Shut up now! Shut your face!"*

Denny refused. He wouldn't let the opportunity pass. He could see she was vulnerable in this moment, that she was either remembering pieces from the past or, at the very least, doubting the life she'd known.

"We loved each other very much," Denny said. "You remember. I know you do. We used to play in the park. You used to ride on my back. You would yell out..."

She looked up at him, a strange look on her face, and said: "Mr Dinosaur."

Denny could feel himself starting to cry. He didn't know if he was producing actual tears, but his eyes were at least making the attempt. *"Yes, Allie, yes! Mr Dinosaur!"*

She stood there staring at him, looking confused, saying nothing. She was trembling, almost violently. Denny knew he'd shattered her conceptions of who she was and what her life was. But she needed to know who she was.

She stared at him through tears, some streaming down her face. *"Denny-Pa?"* she asked, trying to remember.

"Yes!" Denny cried out. *"Yes, yes, yes! I'm your Denny-Pa! You do remember! You do!"*

She stared at him, her mouth agape.

She said it again: "Denny-Pa," as if trying to make sense of it.

She stared at him, her head slightly cocked as though she was working it all out. She nodded, saying nothing. She just kept staring, and for a long moment neither of them said a word.

And then she said, "I remember."

Denny felt a smile touch the corners of his lips.

"You never came for me," she said.

This was the last thing he heard before the swooping ball-peen hammer struck him in the head.

SEVENTEEN

Denny and Allie were back at the park. Denny was somehow aware of the fact that this was a dream, but he embraced it. He didn't know how or why, but he felt the ability to shatter the dream and wake himself. But he chose not to. Deep in the recesses of his mind, he knew what he was seeing was not his reality. But it was the reality he *wanted*, so he went along with it.

It was impossible for Denny to see or know this, but on the exterior of his body, his lips were smiling.

Allie was hanging from the monkey bars, her feet dangling, with Denny standing there to catch her if she fell. "You can do it, baby," Denny was telling her. He couldn't hear sound in the dream, but somehow knew the words. *"No, I can't!"* she cried. But he encouraged her. "Yes you can." And Allie took one of her gripped hands from the bar and moved it towards the next, grabbing it, pulling herself forward.

"I did it," she said, trying not to fall. There was emotion in her words, even if Denny couldn't hear them, and tears in her eyes. Yes, she did it. Denny held his hand on her back, standing

there to catch her, and she proceeded to move forward, swinging from one bar to the next.

The dream cut forward to another scene, still at the park, as though this were a montage. Allie was in the "big-girl swing", which was what she called the swings without the child-protection bars. Denny was behind her, pushing her.

"Higher, Denny-Pa!" she screamed. *"Higher!"*

Denny could see them both in the dream, as he was somehow given an objective view as if watching a film. When he looked, he saw that both he and Allie were smiling. It was a spring day and the plants and flowers were blossoming, and the entire world was gorgeous and green. There was a soft breeze on his skin. Somewhere in the back of his mind, Denny wondered if he could actually *feel* the breeze in the dream, or if he somehow just knew it the way he knew the words being spoken.

The scene was familiar and Denny thought he remembered it, but this might have been a faulty conclusion as there had been many such days, all of which ran together in his mind. Watching the two of them, he remembered how happy they had been. And in that moment, he felt it again.

Suddenly, the scene changed and Denny saw them at Chuck E. Cheese, where he had taken her for her seventh birthday. The last birthday they had spent together. The two of them played arcade games and then watched a show with animatronic animals playing instruments. Denny looked at her, watching the animals perform, and saw that she was overcome with joy.

She turned to him now, and the animatronic music seemed to stop. "I love you, Denny-Pa," she said. "Thank you for bringing me here. This is the bestest day of my whole life!"

Dream or no, the scene and the sentiment warmed his heart. He saw himself embrace the little girl as they sat there.

The scene switched again, this time to their backyard. Allie was up on his shoulders and they were playing the dinosaur game. He was galloping around the yard, like a horse, and she was yelling out, *"Faster, Mr Dinosaur! Faster!"*

He looked at her smile. She was so beautiful and delicate. She...

SUDDENLY, THERE WAS PAIN! UNGODLY PAIN!

The dream snapped. This pain was something outside the dream, in the real world. The pain was extreme and sharp, as sharp as anything could be, and it was in his left eye. He tried to move his hands towards the pain, but found he could not as he was strapped down.

THE GODDAMN PAIN! THE HORRIBLE, TREMENDOUS FUCKING PAIN!

He heard the adult Allie giggle and he opened his eyes, or *tried* to. His right eye opened, blurry at first, but his left wouldn't budge. That was where the pain was, and something was stopping his eye from opening.

Denny heard himself screaming, and the pain was unrelenting. With his right eye, he could see something on the left side of his face. And he realized – *there was something sticking out of his closed eye!*

JUST AS CORDELL HAD REMOVED HIS NOSE, ALLIE – HIS ONCE-LOVING, BEAUTIFUL BABY ALLIE – HAD STUCK A PENCIL THROUGH HIS EYELID AND INTO HIS EYE!

He screamed and cried and bled and hurt, all at once. He couldn't see her, as she was on his left, but he could hear her cackling.

No! No! This couldn't be real. Maybe this was another dream, just a darker, more macabre one. But the pain told him otherwise. He bucked and screamed, fighting against the straps.

"An eye for an eye," she said gleefully, laughing a crazed

laugh. "You killed my daddy! You killed my daddy, and now you're gonna pay! How you like that, Mr Dinosaur?"

"*NOOOOOOO!*" screamed Denny. "*NOOOOOOO!*"

There was nothing else to say, nothing else to scream. Deep down he wondered why this was happening, how a loving God could allow this, but these were not surface thoughts. On the surface all he could think about was the pain. The agonizing, excruciating pain that made him want to die. He couldn't stop screaming, just as Allie couldn't stop giggling. Denny screamed and screamed until finally, at last, he passed out.

EIGHTEEN

Allie had used the blowtorch to burn the gaping hole where his eye had been, and had then stuffed a wad of gauze into it. The damn thing still bled. A lot. The pain was unbearable. Denny could focus on nothing beyond the pain. He now realized the pain he'd felt before when he'd had his finger and nose cut off were nothing compared to what he felt now. On top of all this, those wounds hurt additionally.

Without medication and medical supervision, Denny's time was limited, and he was aware. He welcomed death. He was ready. He'd experienced enough of life and all its pain and he was ready to leave. Not just this basement, but life altogether. He no longer wanted to find a heaven. He wanted no hell, no purgatory. All he wanted was to cease to exist. He was tired of it all.

He was chained again, lying on the floor in the basement, hurting and bleeding. The light was fixed and on again, and the glass had been swept up. He cried intermittently, but tried not to as doing so hurt his gouged-out eye even more. When he could produce a coherent thought and focus on it briefly between the constant pangs of pain, they were thoughts and memories he wanted to avoid. They were thoughts of his Baby Allie and the monster she'd now become. They were contemplations – at least what could be managed in the seconds between excruciating bursts of pain – on the irony of coming to save Allie only to be tortured and killed by her.

When Denny was younger, his father had told him that life wasn't fair. It was perhaps the only solid and true piece of advice George Davis ever gave his son before proving it by treating him and his mother like shit. Life had never been fair to Denny, and he was sick of it. He wasn't bitter. He knew he had every right to be angry, but he wasn't. Not really. He had resigned himself just to take his lumps and die.

But there was one thought that recurred to him during all this, over and over. He would not hurt Allie. No matter what, under no circumstances, would he fight her. Whether she was aware of it or not, she was still his Baby Allie, and he would die her Denny-Pa. Her being aware of his love and sacrifices wasn't as important as the fact they were true. In this one regard, just this one, Denny had done the right thing. He would go to his grave – if he was even lucky enough to receive one – knowing he had died loving his granddaughter, even if she did not love him back.

Looking back over his life in this context, he realized his love had never been reciprocated fully by anyone. Not by his wife. Not by his daughter. Not by his granddaughter. Well, he reminded himself, there was his Timmy. Denny was pretty sure Timmy had died loving his father, even if it was only because he had been too young at the time of his death to have yet developed a hatred for him. Thinking about all this, Denny disliked the notion of being a victim. Denny had failed at most things in life – that fact was quite clear now – but he'd never allowed himself to be a victim. Maybe life had made him a victim by the definition of the word, but Denny had never bowed down and embraced that. He'd never taken advantage of that or sought pity. He had stood defiantly and kept fighting until... death, which seemed near.

Lying there, his ravaged eye facing the floor, there was a puddle of blood beneath his cheek. At times he lost lucidity altogether, and he faded in and out of consciousness. The water bowl Allie had refilled was less than a foot away, but he had made no attempt to drink from it since losing his eye.

He didn't want anything, didn't want to do anything. He was content to just lie here and bleed, waiting for death.

But that wouldn't happen. Not so easily. He knew Allie would not relent. She would not allow him simply to die in peace. Thanks to that fuckhead Cordell, she was now just like him. A younger, prettier version of Cordell with a better lineage, but she was the same. And Denny knew she would prolong his suffering and keep him alive as long as she could.

He wondered what she might cut from his body next. Maybe his ears. Or a leg. Or his dick. The thought of all these things pained him, but he found that he no longer cared. Not really. Because as painful as these things would be to endure, they would bring him closer to his inevitable death. And that was a good thing. Denny was ready to die.

NINETEEN

Allie came bounding down the stairs with a bounce in her step. She was carrying a hunting knife that looked like something from a Rambo movie. She was enthusiastic, the antithesis of what Denny was now. He was lying there, facing the steps, when she emerged.

"Hiya, Mr Dinosaur," she said, mockingly.

Denny said nothing. He didn't feel like playing games. He didn't want to interact with Allie. Just looking at her, realizing what she'd become and what she now signified for him, broke his heart. It broke his everything, completely crushing his spirit and soul. He wanted to cry every time he looked at her soft, delicate features, obscuring something hard and cold beneath.

"You know what you look like?" she asked.

Denny said nothing.

"You look like a sonofabitch without an eye or a nose!" she said giddily. "Missing just one of those things is bad, but both?" She giggled, looking down at him with mock pity. "I hate to break it to you, Mr Dinosaur, but your dating days are over. I've never met a woman who was looking for a guy without a nose.

Maybe some girls will put up with a guy without an eye. You know, there are fake eyes – marbles – for that. Patches, too. Women will even put up with two-minute guys with tiny pricks. But no nose? I'm sorry, but not having a nose is a definite deal-breaker."

Denny lay there, saying nothing, letting her have her fun.

"I know some ugly bitches who are into ugly dudes," she said. "They're not their first choice or anything, but you know, Ryan Gosling doesn't really go for big girls with body odor and a low IQ. But you know what, Mr Dinosaur? Even those bitches won't touch you. Hell, I doubt you'd even be able to get a hooker to touch you without puking. You really are gross."

Denny raised his head, still lying there but with his head off the floor, looking at her. "Why are you doing this? I loved you so much. You loved me. We were a family, Allie. You were my Baby Allie. You were my everything."

She frowned. "*Was I? Was I really?* It seems to me if I meant so much to you, you'd have come looking for me."

"We did look," said Denny. "We looked everywhere."

She stared into his remaining eye. "You didn't look here." Then she laughed, hard, a belly laugh. "Well, I guess that's not true. You're here now. But it's not doing much for you, is it, Mr Dinosaur?"

She was standing before him, his eye facing her sneakers.

"Stand up," she demanded.

He moved, trying to look up again, saying nothing.

She kicked him hard in the stomach. *"Are you deaf, fucker? I said get up!"*

"Why?"

This time she kicked him hard in the face, the tip of her sneaker smashing into his mouth. His head shot back and his mouth hurt. He was pretty sure he lost a tooth, but was too disoriented to know for sure.

"Get the fuck up," she snarled.

He put the palms of his hands flat against the floor, pushing himself up. His body ached – all of it, from his feet to the wounds on his head – but he did it. It was slow, but he rose to his feet, swaying.

"Real tough guy, huh, Mr Dinosaur?"

"Please, Allie."

"Ruth. My name is Ruth."

"Allie," he said.

This angered her and she stabbed him in his belly with the blade, a quick, almost lightning-fast motion. The pain was severe and he doubled over, seeing blood trickling from the wound as he did.

"My name is Ruth, you fuck."

He was still doubled over in pain when she said, "Say it. Say my name, Mr Dinosaur. Say my motherfucking name."

He stood erect again, his abdomen hurting, and he stared into her eyes. "Allie Davis," he said. "Your name is..."

Before he could finish, she stabbed him again, mere inches from the first cut. Denny howled in pain, bending over. He realized he was crying. Staring at the floor, trying to hold his wounds with his shackled hands, he said, *"Please no. No more."*

She laughed a wicked laugh. He wasn't looking at her, as he was still doubled over.

"Say my name, fucker," she said. "Say my name, Mr Dino-fuckin'-saur!"

Still doubled over, he said, "Ruth." There was a silence and he repeated it. *"Ruth.* I said it."

Still looking down, he saw the knife swoop upwards towards his abdomen. Instinctively he moved his arm to block it, and the blade sliced his arm. Now moving on instinct, he batted towards the blade. When he did, his arm struck Allie's torso and the arm holding the knife, and she stumbled back. He straightened a bit, just enough to see her twist and then topple to the floor, falling onto the blade.

She screamed as the knife pierced her chest. Denny heard himself yelp as this occurred. She moved a bit, pulling at the knife lodged between her and the floor, but to no avail. She looked up at him, a confused look on her face. Her eyes were big, staring up at him, and she opened her mouth, blood spilling out as she did.

"You were right," she gasped.

Denny couldn't reach her to console her. She was just out of his reach. "What?" he asked. "Right about what?"

"You said we would be together...*until one of us was dead.*"

Hearing the words horrified him. No. He wouldn't let her die. She couldn't die. But she did. Right then and there. Just as he had been unable to stop his wife and children from dying, he had been unable to save Baby Allie. Even worse, he'd been the cause of her death.

He fell to his knees, feeling them banging hard against the floor. He looked up at the nothing above and screamed, holding up his shackled arms. He screamed and screamed until he could scream no more, crying all the while.

He had killed Baby Allie.

TWENTY

Having wept for hours, Denny sat there staring at Allie's lifeless body. He was thankful he couldn't reach her to eat her if the necessity arose. But just as he could not reach her, he also could not reach the knife to kill himself.

Without food or water, Denny would die soon, but not soon enough. He was tired, exhausted from crying, exhausted from living. He knew he couldn't wait for death to come. He had to force it, had to find a way to take his life. But how? Denny didn't know. He looked around his space for the millionth time, still finding nothing with which he could do the deed.

Then it occurred to him. It might work. Probably not, but it *could*. He stood again, swaying as he did. He looked at the wall, about six feet away. He had to try, he thought. He lowered his head, aiming the top of his cranium towards the brick wall. He took a moment to muster up all his strength and then bolted towards the wall, slamming his head hard into it. The pain was sudden and intense, knocking him down. It did not render him unconscious, but it caused his head to bleed profusely. There was blood in his eye.

He stood again, his head throbbing, feeling as if it might cave in. He lowered his head again, just the same, and bolted into the brick wall once more. He collided, crashing hard, everything going black for a moment, and he fell to the floor, completely disoriented. There was blood all over his face and hands, in his eye, everywhere. His thoughts were a jumble but somehow, he still knew what had to be done. He stood again, swaying, lowering his head, aiming his cranium, and he rushed into the brick wall, knocking himself unconscious this time.

When he awoke, he had no idea how long he'd been out. His head hurt terribly – worse than his other injuries – and his vision was wonky. He was seeing double. There was blood in his eye again. He didn't even bother to wipe it away.

He stood again, lowering his head towards the wall, preparing to bolt into it. He would do this as many times as it took. He had to die as quickly as possible. He *had* to. And in this moment, it occurred to him that he was trying to do exactly what Cordell had wanted him to – die for his sins. He sprinted towards the wall one last time, seeing Baby Allie in his mind's eye. Her smiling face would be the last thing he would ever see.

Dear reader,

We hope you enjoyed reading *Until One of Us Is Dead*. Please take a moment to leave a review, even if it's a short one. Your opinion is important to us.

Discover more books by Andy Rausch at

https://www.nextchapter.pub/authors/andy-rausch

Want to know when one of our books is free or discounted? Join the newsletter at

http://eepurl.com/bqqB3H

Best regards,

Andy Rausch and the Next Chapter Team

Andy Rausch is the author of nearly forty books, including *The Suicide Game*, *Bloody Sheets*, *Riding Shotgun and Other American Cruelties*, and *Layla's Score*. When he's not writing, he's dividing his time between being a family man, a serial killer, and an international man of mystery. He resides in Nowhere, Kansas.

You might also like:
The Suicide Game by Andy Rausch

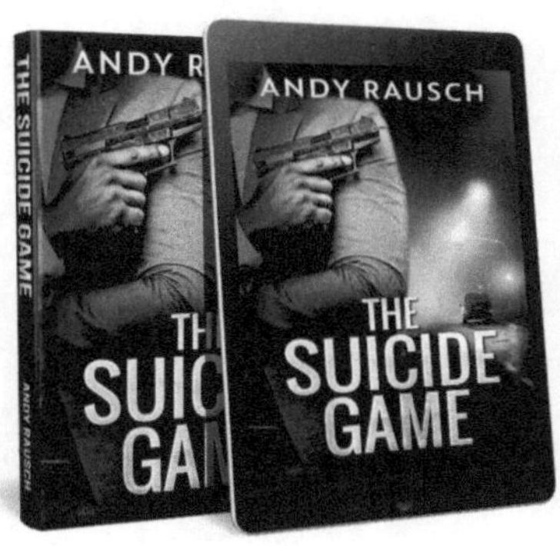

To read the first chapter for free, head to:
https://www.nextchapter.pub/books/the-suicide-game

Until One Of Us Is Dead
ISBN: 978-4-86750-662-2

Published by
Next Chapter
1-60-20 Minami-Otsuka
170-0005 Toshima-Ku, Tokyo
+818035793528

7th June 2021